What the critics say about Harlequin Romances...

"...clean, wholesome fiction...always with an upbeat, happy ending."
—*San Francisco Chronicle*

"...a work of art."
—*The Globe & Mail*, Toronto

"Nothing quite like it has happened since *Gone With the Wind...*"
—*Los Angeles Times*

"...among the top ten..."
—*International Herald-Tribune*, Paris

"Women have come to trust these clean, easy-to-read love stories about contemporary people, set in exciting foreign places."
—*Best Sellers*, New York

OTHER
Harlequin Romances
by ELIZABETH GRAHAM

2062—THE GIRL FROM FINLAY'S RIVER
2088—THE SHORES OF EDEN
2126—FRASER'S BRIDE
2170—HEART OF THE EAGLE

Many of these titles are available at your local bookseller
or through the Harlequin Reader Service.

For a free catalogue listing all available Harlequin Romances,
send your name and address to:

HARLEQUIN READER SERVICE,
M.P.O. Box 707, Niagara Falls, N.Y. 14302
Canadian address: Stratford, Ontario, Canada N5A 6W2

or use order coupon at back of book.

Mason's Ridge

by

ELIZABETH GRAHAM

Harlequin Books

TORONTO • LONDON • NEW YORK • AMSTERDAM • SYDNEY

Original hardcover edition published in 1978
by Mills & Boon Limited

ISBN 0-373-02190-9

Harlequin edition published August 1978

Copyright © 1978 by Elizabeth Graham. Philippine copyright 1978.

All rights reserved. Except for use in any review, the reproduction or utilization
of this work in whole or in part in any form by any electronic, mechanical or
other means, now known or hereafter invented, including xerography,
photocopying and recording, or in any information storage or retrieval system,
is forbidden without the permission of the publisher. All the characters in this
book have no existence outside the imagination of the author and have no
relation whatsoever to anyone bearing the same name or names. They are not
even distantly inspired by any individual known or unknown to the author, and
all the incidents are pure invention.

The Harlequin trademark, consisting of the word HARLEQUIN and the
portrayal of a Harlequin, is registered in the United States Patent
Office and in the Canada Trade Marks Office.

PRINTED IN U.S.A.

CHAPTER ONE

'AREN'T you dressed yet, Cori? For heaven's sake, people will be arriving any minute now.'

Doreen Page, tautly svelte in a beige full-length dress which somehow managed to match the unlikely shade of her hair, regarded her younger sister's reflected image in the dressing table mirror with irritated brown eyes.

There was envy, too, in the gaze that went over Cori's slender shape in a white floor-length slip before going back up to the cascade of light brown hair falling over smoothly young shoulders. The problems Doreen had in keeping her own figure at a reasonable level of slimness were unknown to Cori, whose healthy appetite gave Doreen cause to wince at times.

'Don't fuss,' the younger girl said briefly, getting up after a last frown into the mirror and going to the white louvred doors of a closet stretching across the width of one wall. 'It isn't necessary for me to be there when the guests arrive—in fact, it wouldn't matter if I didn't show at all.'

'It would matter to Howard!' Doreen returned shortly. 'Some of the bank's most important investors will be here tonight.' Her eyes went significantly round the luxuriously appointed room. 'Even you must admit that Howard has been more than generous to you, and the least you can do is——'

'Oh, all right, Doreen!' Cori snapped, sliding a long white sheath dress over her head and turning her back wordlessly for her sister to pull up the zipper to its resting place just below her shoulder blades. 'Howard won't have to provide for me much longer. As soon as my teaching certificate comes through I'll——'

'Don't talk that way—you know very well Howard's been happy to help you with your education, and Mother and

Dad to retire in Arizona. He's never once complained, but I think——'

'I know,' Cori said contritely, her voice softening. 'Howard's a dear—even though he's filthy rich!' Her widely set hazel eyes glinted with laughter at Doreen's outraged expression.

'I don't know what you have against men who are comfortably off.' Doreen drew her shoulders up haughtily. 'It's just as well you've broken off your engagement to Roger—talking about living on a shoestring is a very different thing from actually doing it.'

Cori's smile had disappeared at mention of Roger Hansen, and she sat down suddenly at the dressing table and picked up a brush, drawing it through her hair with long rhythmical strokes as if in that way she could regulate the beat of her heart.

Belatedly realising her tactlessness, Doreen tried to make amends by saying cajolingly, 'Come on, darling, you never know who you might meet tonight. There's a few people coming who've never been to the house before.'

'And they won't be any different from the regulars,' Cori returned resignedly. 'Fair, fat and the wrong side of forty —with wives to match! Anyway, Doreen, I'm not interested in men as such right now. In fact, I might never be interested again.'

Doreen's well manicured hand came down on her shoulder in a brief yet sympathetic gesture that brought unexpected tears to sting the back of Cori's eyes. It would have been preferable to have her sister's more normal critical attitude.

'I know it's not easy for you, Cori, so soon after—— But I've always found it better to mix and mingle if I'm down about something.' Howard's impatient calling of her name made Doreen drop her hand and turn to the door. 'I'll tell Howard you'll be down in a few minutes. He always says you're so good with people, and he counts on you to make these business parties go off well.'

Seeming satisfied with Cori's jerky nod, she went out and

closed the door quietly behind her, leaving Cori to battle fiercely with the tears threatening to overwhelm her. Tears were a feminine indulgence she had seldom allowed herself in the twenty-two years of her life. There had always been a humorous side to the small disappointments in her life, and her sunny nature had dwelt on that rather than brooding.

Until now ... Incredible that it had been only two days ago she had gone to the apartment Roger shared with two other law students and found him alone—except for Angie —in his bed. Shock had rooted her to the floor, the colour fleeing from her face as Roger came towards her fastening a hastily thrown on robe, his own fair-skinned features suffused with embarrassed colour.

'Cori, it's not how it seems,' he began in a voice meant to be reassuring but which came out as a weak defence.

Cori had taken a shuddering breath and managed to get out: 'Of course not, Roger! I'm sure you were just giving Angie a lesson in mouth-to-mouth resuscitation. Maybe you can put this through her nose and pull her to shore!' She drew off the inexpensive ring he had given her and threw it at him before stumbling out of the apartment.

Now as she stared at her own reflection in the mirror she wondered if part of her shocked horror had been due to the fact that she herself had gone to the apartment with a half-formed intention of doing the same as Angie. The quarrel she had had with Roger the previous weekend had centred round the usual topic of her refusal to give in to his demands that they experience the fullness of their love without waiting for the piece of paper stating they had the right to do so. During the sleepless nights following their deepest quarrel yet, Cori had had time to digest Roger's caustic remarks about her Stone Age morality that made her want to wait for marriage before relinquishing her virginity.

Well, she thought sourly as she surveyed the clear hazel-cum-green of her eyes, she was still untouched. She had lost Roger to a more amenable girl, but she herself was the same pure flower of the forest she had always been. The thought gave her little comfort.

Mingling a short time later with the guests sprinkled across the vast off-white carpeted expanse of the Page living room, Cori moved gradually towards the floor-length windows leading out to the shrub-bedecked terrace overlooking the twinkling city lights of Vancouver across the Inlet. The doors stood open to the terrace, and several people were taking advantage of the unusually warm May evening by drifting out to admire the view.

Cori's smiles were automatic as she paused to speak to the ones she recognised from previous parties—clients of the bank Howard, as President, had invited to his home before. The Delaneys, rich in lumber, stopped her and she greeted them with a more genuine pleasure, having appreciated their down-to-earth naturalness at other parties. The smile still lingered in her wide-set eyes as she looked past Fred Delaney's grizzled head into eyes that caught and held her with their blackness. Feeling the bold appraisal there, she turned her back and concentrated on what the older couple said. Male eyes of any colour were of no interest to her now, however appreciative they might be.

Nevertheless, she was conscious of the penetrating dark-eyed gaze on her back, and eventually she turned to look coldly over in the man's direction. There was something almost foreign in his darkness, in the hair that matched the blackness of his eyes and the deeply layered tan on his skin. A white dinner jacket served to emphasise his darkness and did nothing to hide the breadth of shoulder under it. That he was attractive to the women who, with a scattering of men, surrounded him was obvious in the slant of their heads in his direction. A blonde woman close to his side put a hand on his white sleeve and Cori turned away, a faintly bored look crossing her face. If there was anything she wasn't in the mood for at that moment, it was an Adonis with his adoring female public around him.

Howard came to join the group she was with and gave

her a beaming smile which she returned in full. She was fond of her brother-in-law—almost in spite of his generosity to her family—and although he was approaching fifty to Doreen's thirty, Cori wished that his dream of having at least one child would come true. He would make a wonderful, if indulgent, father.

'I was just saying,' Fred Delaney told him with a twinkle in his eyes, 'if this girl ever wants a job in my company it's hers! That smile of hers would charm a bird off a tree.'

'Sorry, Fred, you'll have to stand in line behind me and the School Board,' Howard returned, his arm going round Cori's waist to give it a brotherly squeeze.

'I'm leaving before all this flattery goes to my head,' she inserted, smiling as she detached herself from the group and almost ran into Doreen and the dark man who had been watching her so closely.

'Oh, Cori! Here's someone who's asked particularly to meet you,' Doreen said with an arch smile that told Cori that the man was obviously important, in her eyes at least. 'Gregory Mason—my sister, Corinne Davis.'

'How do you do, Miss Davis.' Cori's five feet seven inches was dwarfed by the man's much taller figure, the hand he put out totally engulfing the fine bones of hers.

At closer range, his tan seemed more deeply etched, the whites of his eyes startlingly clear against irises so dark as to appear jet. Her eyes were drawn up to the place above his temple where a broad white scar gouged the bronzed skin and disappeared into the thickness of his black hair.

Cori felt herself flush when her eyes came back to meet the boldly challenging look in his, a look that dared her to find the total man wanting because of a facial scar. She blinked, then realised that Doreen's voice had been prattling on while she herself had been rudely scrutinising the stranger.

'. . . ranch in the Interior. Though how you can bear to live in such an isolated place is beyond me, Mr Mason,' she ended, turning to give him the full battery of her social smile. 'I like lots of life around me.'

'There's a lot of life around a ranch, Mrs Page,' he returned equably, a glint of cynicism, or amusement, appearing at the back of his eyes. 'Not the kind you're used to, maybe, or the type you'd care much about, but it suits me very well.' His gaze rested briefly on Cori's upturned face. 'Animals make a lot more sense than humans most of the time.'

His voice, pitched neither too high nor too low, held a faint drawl which Cori sensed might be misleading, just as his loosely held figure gave a deceptive hint of laziness. It wouldn't be hard to imagine the smoothly co-ordinated form springing rapidly into action when the occasion demanded.

'You're joking, of course,' Doreen's smile thinned nervously and she added in a hurried tone as if she feared his enlargement on the topic: 'Well, I'll leave you two to get acquainted. I see Howard needs me.'

Cori watched her sister glide over to Howard's side, almost forgetting the tall man by her side until he said:

'Would you like to come outside? We can talk in peace there—you do have a tongue, I presume?'

She blushed again under the light amusement in his voice, feeling vaguely irritated by his air of confident self-assurance. The fingers he put under her elbow to lead her to the terrace were firm and unyielding.

'Yes, I have a tongue,' she told him acidly. 'But as some others have found, it might be a little sharp for your taste.'

As he slowed to a halt, his hand pulled down on her elbow to bring her to a standstill beside him. 'It sounds as if it could be a very—attractive one—if you'd let it be.'

Cori pulled away from his grasp and passed through the doorway to the terrace, walking ahead to stand against the curved top of the balustrade, sensing the figure looming up behind her and wondering why she felt such instant animosity towards a man she didn't know. It was his calm assumption that she would be flattered at his singling her out from the other women for his attention, she decided waspishly. Granted, he had the dark good looks most women found attractive, and the scar did nothing to take away those looks. If anything, it added an air of mystery which some females would find exciting.

The scar was invisible as he sat on the balustrade with his back to the moonlight and took a cigar case from his pocket, asking if she minded if he smoked.

'I don't if you don't,' she said with pointed sarcasm, and vaguely discerned the lift of his thick eyebrows.

'I doubt if one or two cigars a day constitutes a health hazard,' he remarked mildly, his face illuminated in stark clarity when he struck a match and applied it to the slender cigar held between strong white teeth. Everything about him hinted of a strength beyond that of most men she knew. What had Doreen said? That he was a rancher in an isolated interior spot ... which would account for his weather-beaten tan so early in the season. The knowledge lessened her feeling of contempt for the rich playboy she had imagined him to be—yet if Howard had invited him here tonight, he must be wealthy.

'Your ranch ...' she began, faintly curious, '... is it a big place?'

'Big enough,' he replied with a noncommittal shrug. 'I run a few thousand head on it, and some is given over to logging.'

'Oh.' Cori's mind boggled at trying to conjure up a picture of thousands of cows being accommodated on one ranch, and she gave up the attempt. It was of no real interest to her in any case. Her eyes picked out the lights of the city in the background, and her throat closed round a painful lump. Roger was over there somewhere—alone in the apartment—out dining somewhere with Angie? Sudden tears shimmered in her eyes, and she turned away from the intent cast of Gregory Mason's head as he looked across at her, Even though he was half sitting, his eyes were on a level with hers.

'Your brother-in-law told me about your recent ... bad experience,' he said tentatively, his eyes still steady on hers although she gasped and widened her gaze on the blur of his face not far away. 'He also told me you're a teacher.'

'I—I will be when my certificate comes through in a week or so.' She was glad the conversation had taken a turn towards a more impersonal subject, but his next words had her mouth opened unbecomingly as she stared at him.

'It was for those two reasons I came here tonight,' he said, ignoring her last statement. 'I thought you might be interested in a proposition I have to make to you.'

'Proposition?—to me?' Cori's mind swirled in confusion around the central fact that Howard had confided personal details about her life to this stranger. Glinting anger replaced the tears in her eyes. 'I doubt if any proposition you might have would interest me in the least, Mr Mason.'

'Won't you at least hear what it is before turning it down out of hand?' He straightened from the wall and grasped her wrist as she turned quickly away, confirming her suspicion that his lethargic manner was a surface thing. 'Please?'

The word sounded strange on his lips, as if it was one he had not used too often, but she said sharply: 'It seems I have no choice but to listen,' looking down at her imprisoned wrist. Yet at the same time, she knew his grip was light enough for her to disengage it if she wished.

'Let's sit down over here,' he suggested, not waiting for an answer before leading her to a white-topped round table in a far corner where a shaded patio lamp cast a flickering glow over their faces. The few others on the terrace were well out of hearing distance.

'Well, Mr Mason?' Cori asked, her full lips compressed to half their normal soft line. 'There are other people I should be spending time with.' Not that Howard deserved her participation in his business party, she added silently to herself. Her brother-in-law would receive the sharpest side of her tongue she had ever shown him for his disloyalty.

'Howard knows of my intention to monopolise some of your time,' Gregory Mason returned unconcernedly, stubbing out his half smoked cigar in the heavy glass ashtray provided, then leaning forward to say with quiet earnestness: 'At it happens, I'm in Vancouver to look for a teacher I can take back to Mason's Ridge with me. It would be a temporary measure, of course, until the end of the school year in six weeks.'

Cori stared at him aghast. 'What in the world possessed you—and Howard!—to think *I* would want to go to the back of beyond, even as a temporary measure? What is this Mason's Ridge, anyway? You have a town named after you?'

Ignoring the biting sarcasm in her tone, he replied evenly: 'Mason's Ridge is my ranch.'

Her eyes widened to saucers. 'You mean—it's big enough to run to a *school*?'

'There are fourteen ranch children attending the school,' he stated in a businesslike tone. 'I find it more convenient to provide school facilities than to replace men frequently because their wives object to sending the children away for the greater part of the year.' He frowned and looked down at his hands clasped loosely on the table. 'It isn't an easy job to teach such a wide age range, as the last teacher found. That, combined with the isolation, was the reason for her throwing in her hand a week ago.'

'And what makes you think I'd find those conditions any more palatable?' Cori asked in an indignant splutter.

'Only that the experience might be good for you,' he replied smoothly, then shot a calculating look across to her wide-set eyes. 'And that you might find it easier to get over your—trouble—in a totally different environment.' A faint smile lifted a corner of his firmly held, but well shaped, mouth. 'There's nothing like a ride over rough country to shake other things from your mind.'

His reference to her broken engagement inflamed her outraged senses again and she stood up, her delicately shaped nostrils flaring slightly.

'I've no doubt it would in my case, Mr Mason, as I've never been on a horse in my life! And I've no intention of getting on one at this point in time.'

She would have stalked away from him, but he stood and came to tower over her. 'I wish you would think about it overnight before refusing. It's very important to me.'

Against her better judgment she asked: 'Why?' and saw
his jaw push forward determinedly.

'Because I have a boy to bring up. He's just finishing
first grade, and I want him to cover the whole year's work
under a competent teacher.'

Her head tilted back to look into the dark pools of his
eyes. 'Your wife leaves all these arrangements to you?' Yes,
of course she would, she answered herself silently when he
hesitated. Any woman married to such a man would per-
force have decisions taken out of her hands.

'I'm not married,' he said tersely at last. 'The boy I'm
responsible for is my dead brother's child.'

'Oh,' she said, nonplussed, reversing her opinion slightly.
An unmarried man who would take on the upbringing of
his nephew couldn't be all bad! 'And—his mother?'

He frowned and looked up over her head to the distant
lights. 'She travels a lot. It's best for the boy to have a
stable home life.'

His tone of finality precluded the asking of more questions even if she had had any. Cori shifted her stance
slightly and looked in the same direction as his eyes took.
What would it be like to live in a place where no friendly
lights twinkled across the water, where instead of people
there were cows to populate the land? Miles and miles of
blackness in every direction. A shiver ran over her skin,
and he looked down at her bare arms.

'You should go inside, you're cold,' he said as a statement
of fact rather than an expression of concern, and she shivered again when his warm fingers fastened round her arm.
'Will you give me your answer at dinner tomorrow night?'

She looked up into his face as they paused at the terrace
doors. 'I can give you the answer right now, Mr Mason.'

His jaw hardened perceptibly, but he persisted: 'Will
you have dinner with me anyway, Miss Davies?'

The white line of her shoulders lifted slightly in a shrug.
'It won't make any difference, but if you're in need of company ...'

'If it was just company I needed, I wouldn't have to look far, Miss Davies,' he said drily, his eyes lifting to where the blonde woman he had been with was re-entering the living room from the hall, her eyes swivelling round the room as if in search of him. Returning his gaze to Cori, he said in a voice that invited no argument: 'I'll pick you up at seven-thirty. Is there anywhere in particular you'd like to go?'

'Devil of the Deep,' she answered without thinking, saying the first name that came to mind.

With a faint nod of his well groomed black head, he stepped inside the doors and went with an easy, confident stride towards the blonde. Cori looked thoughtfully after him, then, instead of following him into the room, went back to stand at the balustrade again, knowing the coldness she had felt previously had been a reaction to the idea of living in primitive isolation in a cattle kingdom that had Gregory Mason as its head. Still, it would only be until the end of the school year, he had said, a matter of weeks.

Her eyes sparkled coldly over the water to the city that held Roger. Roger who couldn't wait ... Perhaps a few weeks in a totally different environment would lessen the hurt ... might even make Roger miss her.

CHAPTER TWO

GREG MASON drew up before the imposing entrance to the Page house promptly at seven-thirty the following evening, and Cori herself opened the white front door, relieved to see that his suit was a casual tan safari type and not evening dress.

She had dithered between wearing an elaborate long dress or a less formal pale green linen that reached just below the knees. Something had told her that Gregory Mason wouldn't appreciate a dinner date who appeared in slacks, no matter how silky. Then she laughed sourly at herself. He was taking her to dinner with a view to being her future employer, not as a romantic assignation. Romance and the hard-jawed rancher were poles apart. Besides, he had the blonde to fulfil his romantic needs.

His eyes flickered dispassionately over the green dress with its wide self-coloured band cinching her waist to added slenderness and down to her feet in heeled white sandals before coming back to her eyes, made more green by the colour of the dress. Her long brown hair, freshly washed, formed a glossy curtain at either side of her face, and he gave what might have been construed as a faint smile of approval.

'You look very—attractive,' he remarked as he followed her into the spacious hall. His voice sounded as if he might be unused to paying compliments to women, and Cori reflected wryly that he probably considered it compliment enough that he deigned to take a woman out in the first place.

'Have we time for a drink?' she asked, leading him into the library where both Howard and Doreen were exchanging desultory conversation over cocktails before dinner.

'A quick one,' he said, turning back his cuff to look at a watch which would have looked ludicrously big on anyone else but suited his overall largeness.

'Well, Mr Mason, how nice to see you again.' Doreen rose from her chair and came to shake hands, a wary look behind her social smile. She had been flutteringly pleased at breakfast when Cori told her she was having dinner with the wealthy rancher, her face falling into disappointed lines when Cori added drily that he was looking for a teacher, not a wife.

'How are you, Greg?' Howard nodded, moving to the small but efficiently laid out bar on the far wall.

'Whisky and soda, thanks.' He looked at Cori in a proprietorial way that sent a shiver over her skin. 'I've made a reservation for eight, so we haven't much time.'

'I'll be ready by the time you are,' Cori answered, re-

lieved to turn away from those black eyes and their penetrating gaze and pick up her half-finished drink. Normally
she drank little except a little wine with dinner, but she
had felt a need to bolster her flagging courage tonight.
Would Gregory Mason accept her change of mind sar-
donically?—with relief?—suspiciously?

She looked at him now as he chatted, glass in hand, with
Howard. The scarred side of his face was away from her,
and his profile had the clear-cut masculine outlines most
women would find devastatingly attractive. He wasn't
married, he had told her, and she wondered why. He
looked to be in his early thirties, so it was possible an
earlier marriage had been dissolved one way or the other.
She started, realising he was coming across to her purposefully.

'I think we should go.' He looked at her bare arms.
'You'll need some kind of covering for later.'

Cori put down her still unfinished drink and moved towards the hall. 'I have a stole out here.' At the door she
turned to say goodnight to Doreen and Howard, feeling
disturbed as she picked up her white wool stole in the hall.
Doreen's eyes had been more than a little speculative as
she looked across the room at Greg Mason's tall figure
beside her sister. Knowing most of the convolutions of
Doreen's mind, Cori was aware that she was thinking what
a handsome couple they made. But she could forget her
dreams of romance in that direction, Cori thought, glancing
up at Greg Mason's sternly set face. Even if she herself
had been in the market for romance, there was obviously
nothing further from the rancher's mind as he dropped the
stole round her shoulders and took her elbow impersonally
to lead her out to his car.

Surprise widened her eyes as he handed her into the
long silver-grey sports model before going round to slide
his long body behind the wheel. 'Is this *your* car?'

'Why do you ask?' His dark brows gave a quizzical lift
as the engine roared into life.

'Well, I—I'd have thought you would own a more— conservative model.'

His chuckle, and the sudden lightening of his expression, surprised her. 'Possibly I would if I owned a car at all. Unfortunately, I have no use for one at Mason's Ridge. There aren't any roads there to speak of. I rent this one when I'm in town.'

Cori's eyes widened on his profile as the car eased from the driveway and turned with barely leashed power into the street. 'Wh-what do you use for transport on the ranch?' she asked faintly.

'The four-legged variety mostly,' he responded cheerfully, glancing at her after halting at traffic lights. 'We have a landing strip there, so we can always reach the outside that way if we have to.' His tone implied that the necessity to reach civilisation did not arise too often in his scheme of things. Changing the subject abruptly, he said as they moved on: 'I'm glad you suggested a seafood place. I eat as much of it as possible when I'm in Vancouver. It makes a change from beef, which is what we mostly have at the ranch.'

'Oh—good.' Cori lapsed into a pensive silence while he concentrated on negotiating the Lions Gate Bridge spanning the North and South Shores with its lacelike structure. Could she really bear, even for a few weeks, the total isolation his words implied? Her mind refused to accept a place where one couldn't just get into a car and go. Her eyes rested on his steady brown hands at the wheel, guessing that he was also the pilot of the plane used for occasional forays into civilisation. Yet wasn't that what she wanted? A completely different environment in which to lick her wounds? From her imaginary concept of Mason's Ridge, there would be little else to occupy her mind, apart from the teaching of fourteen children.

A pang of guilt went through her as he led her a few minutes later to a table by a window overlooking the harbour where freighters from Japan waited to be loaded and a cruise ship, the first of the season, eased its way towards the dock, its deck a blaze of lights. What would Greg Mason think if he knew that this was a restaurant well known to herself and Roger? At their special table, not far from the one the waiter led them to, Roger had proposed to her.

'Do you like anything in particular, or a general seafood plate?' her companion asked when the waiter had brought menus and discreetly departed.

'What? Oh, I like something of everything,' she said absently, scarcely noticing his fluent order to the wine waiter who appeared at his elbow, recognising only that the wines he ordered were expensive imported brands. How she wished she could be back again in the days when the cheaper wine Roger could afford was as elixir to her! Days that would never come again.

'I'm sorry,' she said, drawing her eyes reluctantly away from the activity in the harbour, realising Greg Mason had said something. His eyes were dark and hard, whereas Roger's were the deep clear blue of a summer sea.

'I asked if you've made up your mind whether or not you'll accept my proposition.' There was a hint of impatience in the stern line of his mouth.

'Oh. Yes, I——'

She broke off when the waiter came to take their order, and when he had departed again she added quietly: 'Yes, I think I will accept your offer, Mr Mason. It—suits me to be out of town for a few weeks.'

He made no immediate reply, and she looked up sharply to see his eyes bent on the tablecloth where he was gouging patterns with the tines of his fork. Irrelevantly the thought went through her mind that many women would have been more than happy to possess the dark sweep of lashes against his tanned cheeks. For a moment she thought he hadn't heard her, but then he looked up and fixed his eyes soberly on hers.

'Would you consider a longer period of time in a different capacity?'

She stared across the white tablecloth uncomprehendingly. 'Longer?—different?' she asked, mystified. 'How much longer?—and how different?'

'For a period no longer than six months,' he said quietly, his eyes holding the wide hazel of hers. 'As my wife.'

'You must be mad,' Cori said in a formless whisper, feeling as if her eyes were about to pop out of their sockets. 'We don't know each other, let alone love ...'

'That's all for the better,' he interrupted coolly. 'Then there would be no complications when the—agreement ends.'

'But why? If you need a wife that badly, there must be dozens of women who——'

'Thanks, but there aren't quite that many,' he corrected with a dry smile that touched only the hard lines of his mouth. 'Those I do know well enough would bring the complications I just mentioned. But between you and me there would be no emotional ties, a ...' He broke off when the waiter came to place oval plates before them, the wine waiter appearing at the same time with sparkling white wine encased in a bucket of ice.

While Greg Mason sampled the wine and nodded briefly to the waiter, who then poured generous glasses for each of them, Cori stared unseeingly down at her plate. The scallops from Digby, Nova Scotia, the pink and white lobster from cold Atlantic waters surrounding the same Province, and the salmon and shrimp from their own Pacific might as well have been pebbles from the beach. Was this a bad dream she was experiencing, one of those nightmares she would awaken from and jeer at herself for half believing? But her dark-browed companion was carrying on with the conversation as if it had never been interrupted.

'It would be a business deal, pure and simple. I need someone to act as my wife for a few months, and you need time to get over your personal problem.'

Cori ran the tip of her tongue across her lips and looked

up at him, a puzzled frown dividing the smooth skin on her brow.

'Why—do you need a wife for just a—few months?'

He lifted his glass and drank, his eyes narrowing as he set it down again. 'My sister-in-law is bringing a custody suit to court in September on the grounds that I can't provide a normal family environment for my nephew.'

Bewildered, Cori's eyes searched his hard-set face. 'But surely, if she's his mother she can provide——'

'She can't!' he burst out explosively. 'She travels all round the world, never in one place more than a week. What kind of life is that for a young boy?'

'Why must she travel so much? Doesn't she want to make a home for her son?'

'Marisa has a career,' he bit off in a bitter voice. 'She's——'

'Marisa Mason—the pianist?' Awe edged Cori's voice as she recalled attending concerts given by the gifted pianist in Vancouver the previous summer.

'Yes. You've heard her play?'

'Many times. Roger and I——' She broke off and bit her lip. If she was ever to get over Roger, she would have to stop thinking of him in connection with every subject that came up.

'Then you'll understand why she can't make a permanent home for Bobby—and why I don't want my nephew to live the life of a nomad,' he continued, ignoring her reference to Roger. 'I believe the courts will feel the same way—if I have a wife.'

'A wife for six months?'

He made a dismissing gesture with his hand. 'I can bring Bobby up without the aid of a wife. It's only the court who feels the necessity for a woman's touch.' He looked down at his own plate, and then at hers. 'Let's forget it for a while and eat this food before it gets cold.'

Amazingly, it seemed he could dismiss all disturbing thoughts at the drop of a hat, and after a moment or two's perplexed gaze at his suddenly active fork she lifted her own, though the half-cold food tasted like marbles in her mouth.

Marriage? To a man she had not even met yesterday afternoon? A marriage of convenience ... until now, that phrase had meant no more than a laughable passage in an old-fashioned book. But that was what it would be—for Greg Mason it would be convenient to have a front cover wife for the purpose of gaining custody of his nephew; for her it would mean the total severance of all ties with Roger. But did she really want that? She looked up in panic at the dark head bent over his plate. No! Going away as a teacher for a few weeks was one thing. Marriage to a stranger was another. Roger would never believe that a man and woman could live together without actually living together ... wasn't that what Greg Mason meant? His eyes lifted suddenly to sweep over her flushed face.

'It—wouldn't be a *real* marriage? I mean ...'

'Don't worry,' he assured her brusquely. 'You'd be as pure at the end of our engagement as you are now, whatever that state may be. I have only one purpose in taking a wife.'

Her startled gasp was cut short by the entrance into the restaurant of a figure only too familiar to her. Roger, accompanied by Angie, made an obvious point of asking for the table Cori had come to think of as being exclusively theirs, and hurt seared her when Roger's fair head bent close to Angie's over the table. It hadn't been a passing physical thing, then. The two gave every evidence of being very much in love, their hands reaching out to clasp together on the white cloth. Cori looked with suddenly hardened eyes into Greg Mason's face.

'All right, Mr Mason. I'll be your—temporary wife.'

If he was surprised, his rock-like features betrayed none of it. Even his voice was flatly noncommittal when he said: 'Good. I think as we're to become man and wife, it might be better if we used Christian names rather than Mr and Miss—don't you think so, Cori?'

Cori drew her gaze away from the loving couple a few tables away and said abstractedly: 'What? Oh, yes—I suppose so. Everyone would think it odd if we——' She stopped abruptly and looked concernedly at him. 'They're going to think it odd if we become engaged the night after we met, aren't they?'

His broad shoulders lifted in a shrug. 'We can leave it a week or so before telling anyone. Everybody knows a rancher doesn't have much time to woo his lady love before the wedding.'

'Doreen will know there's something strange about it.'

'But I gathered from what little conversation I've had with her that she wouldn't object to me as a brother-in-law,' he remarked drily, and Cori's cheeks flamed. Doreen's ambitious matchmaking must be more obvious than she had thought! 'I think even your sister will find nothing to complain about in the settlement I mean to make when our—marriage—breaks up.'

He raised a hand and the waiter came with coffee immediately, but Cori's eyes still sparkled when the man had left them again.

'Money doesn't interest me, Mr Mason,' she said icily. 'I——'

'Greg,' he interrupted smoothly, looking speculatively at her before lifting the sugar bowl and placing it at her right hand. 'I believe you. But I don't expect that you'll do me this big a favour for nothing. I can well afford to——'

'I'd rather not talk about that side of it, Mr Ma—*Greg*!' His name sounded strange on her lips, but then the whole set-up was more than a little strange.

While they drank their coffee and Greg smoked a cigar, he outlined what he thought their plan of action should be for the following week, but Cori heard little of it, her eyes straying several times to Roger's fair head so close to Angie's. When at last she and Greg passed the table on their way out of the restaurant, her heart missed a beat when the familiar voice came from behind.

'*Cori!*'

Roger was on his feet when she turned round, a frown between his light coloured brows when his eyes went past Cori to the tall figure behind her.

'Oh—hello, Roger, Angie. I didn't notice you come in.'

'I've tried to call you, Cori,' Roger said, his voice urgently low. 'Doreen always said you were out. Did you get my messages?'

Cori gave a purposefully breathless laugh and turned to Greg, placing a hand intimately on his arm. 'I'm sorry— I've been busy.'

She introduced Greg, feeling suddenly glad that he was a man any woman would be proud to be seen with, and Angie's dark eyes widened—whether in appreciation of that fact or that Cori had replaced Roger so quickly was unclear, but the effect was enough to soothe Cori's raw feelings. Added balm was the scowl deepening on Roger's brow.

'I think we'd better go, Cori,' Greg put in smoothly, sliding an arm round her waist to urge her forward. 'We seem to be holding up the traffic.'

A waiter was, indeed, endeavouring to pass them and Cori gave the other couple a sunny smile and moved on, scarcely feeling Greg's arm round her in what might be seen as a protective manner. Her eyes blurred with tears as they left the dining room for the foyer. Greg took her stole and draped it round her, letting his hands rest on her shoulders when he said:

'That was your ex-fiancé, I presume—and your replacement?'

She looked up at him with swimming eyes, then dropped her head to nod dumbly. His hands stayed on her shoulders a moment longer, then he put a steady grip on her elbow to lead her to the car.

'I found it encouraging that you were able to lie so successfully about not having seen them,' he remarked conversationally as he bent to unlock her door. 'It means you'll also be able to carry out our little subterfuge better than I expected.'

'How did you know I was—lying?' she gulped when he took his place behind the wheel, and he glanced across at her with a sardonic lift of his brows.

'You have very expressive eyes,' he drawled. 'And it needed very little sensitivity on my part to know that you hardly heard a word I said.'

Silence reigned while he put the key in the ignition, but when the engine came to life she said in a small voice: 'I'm sorry. I—just didn't expect to see them there tonight.'

'Didn't you?' His square-tipped fingers manipulated the wheel so that the car slid easily from the parking lot to join the line of traffic. 'I had the impression you'd been there many times before—probably with Roger—and that you thought you'd see him there or that you would have a chance to indulge in nostalgic memories.'

Her hair swung back from her face as she turned her head to stare at him, her eyes still bright with tears. In the shifting light of street lamps they passed, his profile seemed as firmly set as ever, betraying none of the intuitive acumen she knew he must have to put such a correct interpretation on her motives.

'I—didn't think Roger would . . .' she began huskily before her throat closed on a lump of pain.

Greg's cynical laugh jerked her upright, an angry glint replacing tears in her eyes. 'You must really be a confirmed romantic if you think that young man would treat your trysting place as a shrine in the same way you obviously do!'

Her sharp retort was choked back in her surprise that he had turned off into Stanley Park instead of continuing across the bridge to the Page house. There was something to appeal to all age groups in the thousand-acre park in the heart of the city—golf for the energetic, lawn bowling for the more sedate, a zoo for the children's pleasure, and even secluded walks through the giant cedars for lovers—but Cori thought of none of these things as Greg drove to a parking place bordering the Inlet. Lion's Gate Bridge crossed the water to their right in a sparkle of lights, and the silvery shafts of the moon slanted across the dark grey of the water, but the romantic overtones of the scene were lost on Cori.

'You know nothing about Roger,' she said furiously as if there had been no break in the conversation. 'What gives you the right to judge him?'

Greg sighed slightly and kept his eyes on the moonlit water for a long moment before turning unhurriedly to look at her, his eyes dark pools in the dim light. 'An impartial observer sees a lot more than somebody closely involved in a situation,' he explained patiently. 'Roger struck me as the kind of fellow who'd want to keep his cake and eat it too. The girl'—he shrugged expressively—'would be more obliging than you . . . in certain respects.'

Cori gasped at the accuracy of his summation, particularly in regard to Angie, but nevertheless looked furiously away from him. 'Angie has done nothing that I—wasn't prepared to do myself,' she told him with bald truth. 'It was just that she——'

'Got in first?' he supplied for her when she paused, his mouth barely repressing a smile: 'Doesn't that tell you something about your young man's character?'

Her eyes glinted against his in the soft light, then went over the granite outline of his pronounced cheekbones and determined chin.

'Yes, it tells me something,' she snapped. 'It tells me he's a man, with all a man's normal feelings. Feelings you obviously know nothing about, Mr Mason!'

His breath drew in on an audible hiss and his eyes narrowed to gleaming slits as he regarded her. For long moments he seemed not to trust himself to speak, and Cori felt a vague twinge of fear along her spine. At last he said, his voice purposefully even:

'Controlling male urges doesn't mean one doesn't know anything about them, Miss Davis. Don't be deluded into thinking that because I'm taking a—pseudo-wife—I'm incapable of normal masculine responses to an attractive woman. It so happens that at this time I have no wish to complicate matters with the usual emotional entanglement a normal marriage would involve, which is why I've chosen you for the part. At the end of the six months, you'll be free to fade out of the picture without complication. I'll have what I want, and with luck you'll have recovered from what I think is misguided heartache.'

His head had turned to stare across the Inlet while he spoke, but now he turned back to her with bleak eyes. 'And speaking of that, I'd be glad if you'd confine any future outbursts of tears to your solitary pillow. Brides are traditionally happy and smiling, not eating their hearts out over lost lovers!'

Cori's indignant gasp was lost in the roar of the engine as his long fingers turned the key in the ignition. How could she have agreed for one moment to marry this boor of a man, to contemplate going to live in the frightening isolation of wilderness country with only him for company? She said nothing, though, until he had pulled up at the Page front door and turned off the engine.

'I'm sorry, Mr Mason,' she said then with quiet dignity. 'I've changed my mind. I can't go through with a deception like that—letting Doreen, Howard, my parents think it's a normal affair ...'

'I'm not offering you an affair, I'm proposing marriage,' he shot back harshly, his eyes directed to the gravel drive in front of them. 'Would they have been happier if you'd moved in with your fiancé?'

'For heaven's sake,' she cried irritably. 'I'm twenty-two —most girls at my age have been ...' She broke off and chewed her lower lip with angry pressure.

He turned then to look at her, the hardness gone from his features. 'But you're not most girls, are you, Cori? Rightly or wrongly—I'm not saying which—you've been brought up to dream about orange blossom and a white wedding dress that really stands for purity. Some man will be glad of that one day.'

'Really?' she mocked in reaction to the strong feelings his words conjured up. 'After I've been married to you for six months?'

'The marriage will be annulled on grounds of non-consummation,' he said quietly. 'You're young enough not to miss six months out of your life ... and maybe at the end of that time you'll be a better judge of men's characters than you are now,' he added, a caustic note creeping back into his voice.

'I could use that six months to get Roger back,' she said almost to herself, and heard him sigh heavily.

'I'm sure you could—if that's what you want. With the connections your brother-in-law has, you'd be a worthwhile wife for a struggling young lawyer!'

Cori's fists clenched in her lap. 'The more I see of you, the more I dislike you, Greg Mason!'

He shrugged. 'I'm not out to win any popularity contests. All I'm interested in right now is in getting custody of my nephew.'

'Well, don't count on me to help you out!' Cori snapped, throwing open her door and jumping out before he could do more than get swiftly from the car and look at her across the silver-grey top.

'I think you will when you've thought it over,' he drawled at last in his laconic way, infuriating her: 'I'll pick you up at the same time tomorrow evening. This time *I'll* choose our eating place, so wear something a little more dressy, please.'

It was more of a command than a request, and Cori slammed the car door with a crash that reverberated round the rhododendron-lined drive.

'Like hell I will!' she called over her shoulder as she ran up the front steps.

CHAPTER THREE

DESPITE her flagrantly thrown words to Greg Mason, Cori was ready and in the library at seven-fifteen the following evening, the willowy slenderness of her figure shown to advantage in a close-fitting cream sheath dress.

Howard and Doreen had gone to a banking convention dinner, Doreen's brown eyes sparkling the words Cori's detached manner precluded her saying aloud. The fact that Greg Mason was taking her sister to dinner for the second evening in a row seemed highly significant to her, and as Cori paced nervously up and down the library she reflected that perhaps that was just as well. The announcement of their engagement and speedy marriage would come as no surprise to her. That was if Greg turned up at all after their last exchange, she told herself wryly, and went to pour herself a generous portion of the Martini Howard had left in the mixer. Whatever else Greg Mason did for her, he had the distinction of being the first man to make alcohol a little more palatable to her normally abstemious taste!

Yet was it Greg, or the interview she had had a few hours ago with Roger? Wandering over to the unlit fire, she stared pensively down at the logs laid ready for burning at the touch of a match. With Howard out on the golf course for his regular Sunday afternoon game and Doreen resting in preparation for the evening ahead, Cori and Roger had been able to talk in peace in the library—if the angry words they had exchanged could be called 'peace'.

Like a tableau unfolding before the dark background of the grate, she saw again Roger's flushed face, heard his voice telling her earnestly that Angie meant nothing to him, that he had never wanted to marry anyone but Cori.

'I don't know how it happened ... with Angie, I mean,' he said miserably. 'She was just there, I guess, and ... I was mad because of the row we'd had, you and I, the weekend before. It was just one of those things ... it didn't mean anything, Cori, I swear.'

'And what about the hand-holding bit at the restaurant? —at *our* table?' Cori flashed, hurt lifting her voice to a higher pitch. 'That didn't mean anything either, I suppose.'

His eyes seemed bluer suddenly as his colour deepened. 'Angie suggested going there, and I didn't see why not— hell, Cori, I'd been trying to get in touch with you and you wouldn't answer the phone. I thought it was really over, but——'

'And Angie was still available, wasn't she?' Cori mocked bitterly. 'Well, it *is* all over, Roger, and I'm glad I found out the way it would have been if we'd married. At the first sign of a disagreement between us you'd have run off to the nearest woman for comfort.' Her lips pressed together tightly to stop the tears welling up in her throat. 'At least this way Howard won't have the trouble of helping you in your career,' she forced out waspishly at last, part of her longing to hear Roger deny that Howard's influence with leading law firms in the city had anything to do with his relationship with her. Instead, he said:

'I suppose you'll make damn sure I get no help from that quarter! What's the saying? "Hell hath no fury like a woman scorned"—that just about sums you up, doesn't it, Cori?'

'No, Roger, it doesn't,' she disagreed with sudden weariness, her heart like lead in her breast. 'I—I've met somebody else, someone who——'

'It didn't take you long to replace me, did it?' he sneered. 'I suppose you mean the guy you were with last night. From the looks of him, he won't take time to bother about rings before making a passing shot at that precious virtue of yours.' He gave a snide laugh. 'I guess he doesn't know yet that it's a waste of time.'

Cori's hand flew in an arc and contacted resoundingly the smooth side of his jaw, and in another minute Roger had stormed from the house.

Now, as she waited for Greg to arrive, no trace remained of the tears she had shed so bitterly during the afternoon. Her eyes, expressive as the rancher had perceptively noticed, held a sadness in their hazel depths, but her softly moulded chin had the firmness of determination in its rounded lines. A determination to put Roger from her mind, if not from her heart. Would she ever be able to do that? For so long now he had been the centre of her universe, the man she had expected to spend the rest of her life with.

Marriage to Greg Mason and a totally new environment would occupy her surface thoughts, but what of the long days and even longer nights when she was alone and at the mercy of memory? Memories of Roger's laughing face, of the sparkle in his blue eyes dimming to seriousness when he bent to kiss her, of her own breathless anticipation of those kisses. What a fool she had been not to give in to his persuasive urgings long ago! Tonight she might have been deliriously happy, instead of contemplating marriage to a man she scarcely knew.

She put down her empty glass and moved to answer the doorbell, which rang promptly at seven-thirty. At least Greg Mason was reliable as to time . . .

'All right?'

Cori glanced across at her very new husband and nodded dumbly, thankful for the engine noise in the plane which made protracted conversation difficult. Whether from the penetrating roar of that, or from the strain of going through with the elaborate wedding Doreen had insisted on that morning, her head was beginning to throb with a dull ache.

Her eyes lingered momentarily on Greg's carved profile, stark against the hyacinth blue of the sky outside the small plane. She noted the deepened lines of stress round his firm mouth and eyes, and reflected in surprise that the day must have been a strain on his nervous system too. He had been so coolly self-contained and seemingly master of the unusual circumstances of their brief 'courtship' and hurried wedding plans that she had thought him immune to the doubts that had plagued herself.

She admitted honestly in her mind that she had not given

one thought to his reactions to taking part in the charade—
a part he had played with consummate skill, even to the
raising of indulgent sighs when he had lifted his head after
kissing her at the altar, a half puzzled look in his black
eyes, then bent to kiss her again more lingeringly. His lips
had felt hard against the petal softness of hers, the faint
odour of cologne on his skin mingling in her senses with the
massed flowers adorning the altar.

Now she wondered if, like herself, he had dreamed of
marrying someone far removed from a person he hardly
knew, a bride he had taken as a matter of convenience. Because he wanted to keep his dead brother's child close to
him. A child she would be meeting soon when they landed
at Mason's Ridge. How would he, and the rest of the
community at the remote outpost, accept her? From Greg's
noncommittal answers to her partially disinterested questions, she had gathered that there was a housekeeper, Ellen
English, a native Indian woman who seemingly devoted her
life to taking care of the Mason household.

To Cori's half fearful enquiry as to how primitive life
actually was in the vast hinterland, Greg had merely given
a tight smile and an enigmatic: 'We find it adequate.'

Even Doreen's anxious quizzing had elicited little more
from him, and worry about her younger sister's creature
comforts had taken the edge off her pleasure at Cori's capture of the well-to-do rancher. Greg's quiet: 'You and
Howard will have to come and visit us later in the summer,'
did little to appease her apprehensions, and she had looked
worriedly at Cori while she changed into the pale lemon
pants suit she had chosen to travel in.

'Cori, remember that if you find it unbearable there,
you've only to get in touch with us and——'

'And you'll snatch me away from Greg Mason?' Cori
asked wryly, touching up her make-up with deft fingers.

'Well——' Doreen seemed nonplussed. 'He's a very
masterful man and all that, but you're my little sister, Cori,
and you know Howard and I——'

'I know, darling,' Cori turned to hug her sister impulsively. 'Believe me, you'll be the first to know if I need help.'

Doreen's eyes misted over. 'Well, now that Dad and Mother are so far away, and Dad's illness is keeping them from coming to your wedding, Howard and I feel—responsible for you. We don't want you to be unhappy in any way, Cori.'

Cori repressed an involuntary smile now as she looked at Greg's confident hands on the plane's wheel, the long length of him exuding masculine strength and invulnerability, and knew that Howard's portly, middle-aged figure was nowhere near a match for Greg's lean and hardened frame, however unhappy Cori might be.

'We're coming in to the Ridge now,' Greg said, barely suppressed excitement colouring his voice.

Cori wished she could have felt at least a modicum of the enthusiasm he displayed for the beautiful but wild country they had passed over. But perhaps one had to have been born and bred to the remote wilderness to feel that sense of belonging and anticipation. For herself . . .

'There's Mason's Ridge,' he pointed with pride to the stark outline of yellow rock jutting up against the skyline. As they drew closer, Cori saw that the ridge enclosed a valley of almost unnatural greenness, the colour being pointed up by the molten silver of a river snaking its way alongside the verdant pastures to disappear as a thin wraith far ahead.

A small landing strip lay to their left, and Greg took the plane further down into the valley before banking and coming in to land there. Cori drew in a jumbled impression of houses and ranch buildings huddled to one side of the jagged ridge, and on a plateau halfway to its summit a ground-hugging house of impressive proportions.

Greg caught her round the waist to help her to the ground, his hand remaining there as she took in her first breaths of pine-scented air. His eyes had a watchful look about them as they bent to her upturned face.

'Welcome to Mason's Ridge,' he said quietly, keeping

one arm round her when a fresh-faced younger man came round the plane to meet them. Almost as tall as Greg, his lightly bronzed face was split into a welcoming grin as he held out a hand to Greg and eyed Cori with undisguised approval.

'Good to see you, Greg,' he smiled, and looked expectantly towards Cori.

'Cori, this is Hank Iverson, the ranch foreman—my wife Cori, Hank.'

'It's a real pleasure to meet you, Cori,' the surprisingly young foreman told her, enveloping her slim fingers in one of his rawboned hands. 'We've all been wondering what the new Mrs Mason would be like, but I see now we had no need to worry.'

'Thanks—thank you,' Cori stammered, feeling a twitch of irritation because Greg had not told her he had informed the ranch people of their marriage.

'You'll have a chance to meet Cori properly tomorrow,' he said now. 'Right now, she's tired after a long day.'

Cori looked up at him from the loose circle of his arm, wondering vaguely at his perceptive understanding of how she felt, but knew from the withdrawn look about his face that his main concern was to keep her away from the ranch hands and their wives until she had had time to assimilate the role of boss's wife.

'Sure, Greg,' Hank returned cheerfully. 'The jeep's right over there. I'll get your luggage and drive you up to the house.' He reached inside the plane and extracted two of their suitcases, pausing to give Greg a puzzled look when he said:

'No, I'll drive. We'll drop you off on our way.'

'Oh. Oh, yes, sure.' Hank's brow cleared and he grinned. 'Guess you want to show your bride her new home yourself.'

Greg brought out the remainder of their luggage and Cori followed the two men to a jeep standing at the edge of the landing strip, watching as they stowed the luggage in the rear. Greg handed her into the front passenger seat and

Hank waved them off, saying he would put the plane away and walk back.

'Oh, please don't do that,' Cori protested. 'It seems such a long way.'

'Only to your city eyes, honey,' Greg said smoothly, getting behind the wheel. 'We're used to distances here.'

Hank waved cheerfully and turned back to the plane as Greg started the high-pitched motor and set the jeep into motion. Cori glanced at his set face, a sparkle lighting her eyes.

'That wasn't a very nice thing to do,' she remarked edgily, and his faint shrug infuriated her further.

'Hank doesn't mind—why should you?'

'He was good enough to come down and meet us. The least we could do——'

'I pay him to do things like that,' he interrupted brusquely, and she subsided into the hard seat back. Certain that he had discouraged Hank from coming with them because he was unsure of her being able to play her part correctly, she wondered bleakly if he intended keeping her a prisoner in the high-set house which was coming ever closer.

Seeing it at closer range, Cori was impressed with its understated design of simple elegance ... modern, with vast expanses of glass along the front and two end wings set into dark brown wood, yet seeming to blend in comfortably with its surroundings. Although the sweeping structure seemed to hug the ground, dormer windows set into the low-hanging roof indicated an upper storey.

'I thought you said there was no wheeled transport,' she said accusingly after another moment.

'I believe I said that *most* of our transport was of the four-legged variety. We use the jeep for around the buildings and out on the flat.'

Flat! Even though he was driving with maddening slowness, Cori was being tossed about like flotsam in her seat. Curiosity overcame her discomfort, however, and she asked:

'How did you get it here if there aren't any roads? And all this?' She waved a hand that encompassed the house and ranch buildings below and to one side of it.

'What couldn't be brought in by air was floated down the river to a point up there beyond the Ridge,' he explained. 'The rapids start after that point, so the freight was brought by wagon from there. As you'll see, quite a few trips had to be made to build and furnish the main house alone.'

'Yes. It looks—adequate,' she agreed, giving him a sideways look and seeing the faint smile he allowed himself.

'I didn't want to build up a wrong impression. It's still far from the standards you're used to.'

Now she looked fully at him, her eyes large as she realised for the first time how little he knew about her background. Yet how could he, after such a short acquaintance? He hadn't asked, and she hadn't told him that her upbringing had been in surroundings far removed from the luxurious home Howard had provided for her since her parents' retirement a year ago. But now wasn't the time to tell him, and she turned her eyes back to the house nestled on the hill almost immediately above them now.

Anxiety pangs caught her again as Greg swung the jeep to the right and began the ascent up a winding track. How could they hope to carry off such a deception with people who knew him well? Deluding her own family and friends with a speedy courtship and hurried wedding had been one thing. Living a lie for months in close proximity to his nephew and employees was another.

The cluster of buildings and corrals were left behind as they went slowly up the wide earth track towards the house, and Cori gave an involuntary gasp of pleasure when she saw the undulating plains reaching to the far distance where purple-shrouded mountains cast a protective line across the other end of the vast valley. Steep tree-clad hills enclosed one side of the flat, while more gentle slopes rose at the other.

She could see why Greg had built his house here, where he was master of all he surveyed. Although he had been uncommunicative on questions touching his personal life, in the three weeks she had known him she had become aware that he was a man who would take his right of possession as a natural thing. As he was doing now in going to the extreme of taking a wife he cared nothing for in order to retain his hold on his nephew. How far would he go to keep at his side the woman he loved?

Lost in these thoughts, she was startled when Greg said in a quietly possessive voice: 'We're home,' and she realised that the jeep was parked in front of the brown house, which seemed even more impressive now that its glitter of full-length windows was close to hand.

One half of the white-painted double doors leading into the house opened and a plumpish Indian woman of about thirty, her dark hair bound in braids round her head, stepped on to the porch and looked with a pleased smile at Greg before turning more tentatively to Cori. Brown eyes went nervously over the long brown hair and yellow pants suit before coming to rest on Cori's hazel eyes. What she saw there must have pleased her, for her smile widened in welcome as Greg came round to help Cori from the jeep.

Cori had a confused impression of tables and chairs in rustic redwood spaced at intervals along the wide porch before Greg introduced her to the housekeeper.

'This is Ellen English, Cori—she's taken care of all my needs for a very long time.'

'Hello, Ellen,' Cori smiled, and held out a hand which the older woman clasped in both of hers, her plump face beaming.

'About time the boss took a wife,' she said, laughing up into Greg's face when she had scrutinized Cori's. 'Now you'll be filling all these empty rooms with fine sons, take over ranch when you're too old.'

Colour ran hotly under Cori's skin and she glanced up at Greg, wondering if his embarrassment would match hers, but the half smile remained on his lips and his eyes were steady on hers as he said:

'We need time to be together first, Ellen, before we start

filling the house.' He frowned as if in sudden remembrance and turned his head to the housekeeper. 'Where's Bobby?'

Ellen's smile faded and she looked half apologetically at Cori, then back to Greg.

'He went up to his room. Felt shy, I guess.'

'Shy? That's never been a problem before.' Greg seemed unusually agitated, but when he pressed Cori forward into the house she laid a hand on his arm and said softly:

'Don't force it, Greg. Let him come in his own time. Our marriage must have been—a shock for him.'

Greg's dark eyes looked down at her for a long moment before he nodded shortly. 'Maybe you're right. I'll show you around a bit first, then while you're getting settled in I'll have a word or two with Bobby.'

Ellen slid away to the back of the square hall, glancing up to the wrought iron staircase on her left as she passed, as if expecting to see the recalcitrant Bobby there. Greg's hold tightened on Cori's elbow as he led her to a room on their left across the hall's rust-coloured tiles.

'The dining room,' he said, retaining his hold on her arm as his own eyes went appreciatively to the big round table in the centre of the room, the intricately carved buffet along one wall. The other walls were made of glass, one encompassing the view to the front, the other leading to a terraced area at the side of the house where a good-sized swimming pool lay sparkling in the late afternoon sun.

'A *swimming* pool?' Cori gasped, looking up at him with a half reproachful glance before going back to feast on the inviting blueness.

'You like swimming?' Her surprise seemed to please him, and his eyes softened to a molten darkness as a smile played round his lips.

'I love it!' she said with an enthusiasm that had been lacking so far. 'I just never thought—I never imagined——'

'Oh, we're not as uncivilised as you city people think,' he told her drily, coming to stand beside her again, his arm almost touching her shoulder as they stood together looking out at the glittering water. 'We don't have a lake handy for swimming and the river's usually too cold, so I had this put in.'

'I'm glad you did,' she breathed without looking at him. 'That's one thing I'm going to enjoy here.'

After a moment's silence she looked up and surprised an odd expression in his eyes.

'That's all you think you'll enjoy?' he asked reservedly. 'Are you having regrets about our—bargain?'

It was the first time he had asked her such a thing, seemingly having taken it for granted that she would comply with his wishes, and a stab of irritation shot through her as she looked out to the pool area again.

'It's a little late to have regrets now, isn't it?' She laughed shakily. 'I mean—I'm here, and there's no way I can get away unless you take me.'

'You think you might want to get away?'

She shrugged her shoulders to signify her helplessness. 'I just don't see how this is going to work, Greg. These people'—her hand waved in an aimless arc—'they know you. They'll be able to tell in a minute we're not in love with each other.'

Again he was silent, and she gave him another upward glance, feeling a pang of compunction when she saw the deeply bitten lines of strain round his mouth and eyes. He must care deeply about his nephew to have embarked on such a crazy scheme in the first place.

'Maybe you can pretend I'm—what's his name?—Roger,' he said harshly, freezing her compassion instantly.

'And who will you have in mind for *your* pretence?' she mocked. 'The woman you built this house for?'

She heard the sharp inhalation of his breath, but kept her eyes resolutely to the front, her hair forming an impenetrable curtain beside her face.

'Yes, I'll do that,' he agreed heavily, and paused. 'I'll show you to your room now. You can see the rest of the house later.'

Cori hardly noticed that this time he didn't take her arm, instead walking a little ahead of her across the hall to a wide passage branching off at the far end of it. Relief had flooded through her that she was apparently to have her own room, a place where she could be herself without the necessity of acting a part that was becoming more impossible by the minute. Although the marriage was in name only, she had had some misgivings about perhaps having to share, for appearances' sake, a twin-bedded room with the taciturn rancher.

Greg's long strides quickly covered the distance between the hall and master suite layout at the furthest end of the ground floor. The delicate arch of Cori's eyebrows lifted when he opened a door and led her into a completely separate wing of the house, a secluded area which would ensure the utmost privacy for its occupants. Three doors opened off a small hallway, and Greg turned the handle of one to their right and pushed the door open, standing aside for her to precede him into the room.

Words rose and remained trapped in Cori's throat. The room, obviously meant to be the master bedroom, was exquisite in every detail. White shag carpeting completely covered the floor, and the furniture was white too, with gold scrollwork embellishing its edges. Contrasting vividly with the virginal whiteness was the wide bedspread of bright scarlet and tub chairs covered in the same shade. The furthest wall was mostly of glass, and Cori could see why when she moved over the thick rug towards it. The whole valley was spread out below in a kaleidoscope of colours and textures, distance meaning nothing as one blended into the other.

'Oh, Greg, it's beautiful,' she said softly, not turning from her stance at the window. 'You ... must have loved her very much.'

The silence behind her was so profound that she spun round, expecting to find him gone, but he still stood just inside the door, the same odd expression in his eyes that had been there in the dining room. So the cold edge to his voice came like a douse of icy water on her skin.

'I'll get your luggage so that you can get settled in.'

'Thank you.' So he didn't want to talk about the woman in his life, Cori thought, giving a mental shrug. It meant nothing to her. But she crossed to where Greg had been standing to say as he looked back from the small hallway:

'Where do you——? I mean, I hate to put you out of your room ...'

A dry smile faintly lit his eyes. 'I sleep over there,' he pointed to a door opposite. 'I've never used this room.'

'Oh.' Saving it for the special bride he hadn't married after all. Cori wondered why he had taken such care to create a room of startling romantic luxury and then not married when it came to the point. Had the girl changed her mind, had an accident, even died? The remote look on his harshly drawn features stopped her voicing her curiosity, but he seemed to divine her thoughts anyway.

'Our bargain doesn't include baring our souls to each other,' he said stiffly, turning away. 'I'll get your cases.'

His prepossessing shoulders, outlined in the dark suit he had worn for their wedding ceremony, disappeared and Cori turned back into her own room with a sigh, suddenly feeling the tension headache she had experienced earlier turn to tiny hammer blows at her temples. The next few months as Greg Mason's wife loomed as insuperable obstacles in her tired brain, which reasoned that she should have thought more deeply about the commitment she was making before tying herself down to an impossible situation. Even Bobby, Greg's nephew, appeared to have greater reservations about the unlikely union than she herself had.

Greg returned with her cases, setting them on the padded chest at the bottom of the bed.

'I'll bring your trunk in later,' he told her as he straightened up. 'We have supper at seven.'

'Will Bobby——?'

'No, he won't be joining us. He has his meal at six with Ellen. But for tonight ...' He hesitated and Cori inserted quickly:

'You'd like him to eat with us?'

'No. But I'd like you to come to the living room when you're ready, and you can meet him properly.'

'All right.' Cori paused uncertainly before adding: 'What should I wear? I mean, do you change for dinner or what?'

His eyes flicked over her neatly fitting pants suit, then came blandly up to her face again. 'You might feel more comfortable in a dress. Slacks are fine for many activities, but I don't happen to feel they're suited to the dinner table.'

Cori gave an involuntary glance to the view beyond the windows. What could it possibly matter what she wore for dinner in such isolated surroundings? As she had sensed before, however, Greg Mason evidently liked his women to appear feminine, even if there was only himself to see it.

It was almost an hour later when Cori ventured out into the passage and opened the door into the main part of the house. She had unpacked her clothes and hung them in the spacious closets lining one wall of the master bedroom, and taken a soothing shower in the well-appointed bathroom obviously meant to serve both bedrooms of the master suite.

Hesitating between a plain brown dress and a multi-coloured shift, she eventually decided on the more conservative brown, reasoning that Bobby would trust a soberly dressed new aunt more than a flamboyantly bright young woman.

She found her way back to the main hall and turned her steps to the room opposite the dining room, pausing on the threshold to gaze in wordless wonder at the gracious sweep of coffee-coloured carpet which provided a resting place for furniture of differing periods, yet all seemed to blend into one harmonious whole. The honeyed tones of Colonial maple mingled with the elegant sweeps of French Provincial and ultra-modern wrought iron bookcases and spiral floor lamps, giving a tasteful overall effect to the whole room.

Dominating the room, at a spot close to the floor-length windows, was a magnificent grand piano, and Cori thought involuntarily of the problems Greg must have had to bring it upriver to the luxurious eyrie perched on a plateau in the middle of nowhere. Her steps took her across the thick carpet to the ebony black of the piano and her fingers curled round the edge of the closed top. Did Greg himself play, or was this a concession to Marisa Mason's visits to see her son? The thought of the famous pianist visiting the ranch while she herself enacted the part of Greg's wife disconcerted Cori, and she started when a voice came from the other end of the room.

'Cori? I'd like you to meet my nephew, Bobby.'

Cori swung round, her eyes going first to Greg's tall figure, then to the dark-haired boy at the end of his arm, which was laid firmly on the slight shoulders. Her breath drew in in wonder when the boy raised his head to look in her direction before plunging it to the region of his chest again. He was so like Greg in the darkness of his hair and eyes that he could almost have been his son. The brothers must have been remarkably alike in physical appearance, she thought involuntarily, going over to where Bobby stood silently with Greg.

'Hello, Bobby,' she said softly as she drew close to them. 'I've heard a lot about you from your uncle.'

The boy's head remained close to his chest, and Greg's fingers tightened visibly on his shoulder.

'Say hello to your new Aunt Cori,' he said, a slightly menacing note in his tight voice, and Cori looked swiftly up at him in mute warning.

'Hi,' Bobby said in a childish treble, darting a fleeting look upwards to her face and dropping his head again instantly. His eyes were a lighter brown than Greg's, she saw now, his hair several shades removed from the jet black of his uncle's.

'Aunt Cori,' Greg prompted persistently, ignoring her anguished look in his direction. There was something almost pathetic in the young boy's drooping figure in worn blue jeans and striped short-sleeved top. His arms were like olive-skinned spindles, and Cori thought irrelevantly

that Greg himself must have looked like Bobby when he
was a small boy.

'Aunt—Cori,' Bobby repeated obediently but with reluctance, looking up in amazement when Cori's light laugh
encircled the three of them.

'Oh dear, Bobby,' she said breathlessly, 'that sounds an
awful mouthful, doesn't it? Do you think you could manage
just plain "Cori" better?'

Now it was her turn to ignore Greg's disapproving
drawing down of his brows. Bobby was regarding her with
the beginning glimmer of a surprised smile in his eyes.

'Come over here and tell me about the ranch,' she suggested, not touching him but moving over to the U-shaped
sofa in rich brown velvet arranged before the pink rock
fireplace spanning the far end of the room. 'I'm a green-
horn when it comes to ranches, and I'm going to have to
rely on you to put me straight on lots of things.'

She held her breath in the pregnant silence that followed,
a friendly smile remaining on her lips as she looked across
to the big man and small boy, both having slightly bemused expressions on their faces as they regarded her.
Bobby turned his head to look up at his uncle and seemed
reassured by the smile hovering round his lips. Hesitantly,
he moved across the room and took a seat several spaces
removed from Cori, looking assessingly at her when she
said to Greg:

'Do you think you could find us something cool to drink,
Greg? I'm parched after that long plane ride!'

The dark eyes met hers and seemed to convey a message
of thanks before Greg moved over to the small bar just
inside the room. When he came back a moment later to
hand Cori a tall glass topped with ice chips and one to
Bobby that had bubbles rising rapidly to the similarly iced
surface, he said quietly:

'I'll go and change for dinner while you two get acquainted. See that—Cori—has everything she needs, son, will
you?'

Bobby nodded, and as soon as his uncle's broad form had

disappeared asked shyly: 'Would you like some nuts ... or crackers ... or anything?'

'No, I think I'll wait for dinner, thanks,' Cori returned, her eyes falling on the beautiful piano by the window. 'I've heard your mother play at a concert in Vancouver.'

For the first time, light cast a luminous glow in the boy's eyes. 'Have you?' he asked eagerly, then his small mouth compressed as if to conceal a tremble. 'I—I've never heard her play at a concert.'

'Oh, but surely she plays on this lovely piano when she comes to see you?'

'Yes,' he admitted reluctantly. 'But I've never heard her play at a real concert.'

There was wry humour in Cori's: 'Well, I'm sure all the people who pay money to hear her would be more than happy to have her play for them alone, as she does for you.' She paused. 'Does your mother come here often?'

The disillusionment in his adult shrug went to her heart. 'Not very often—she plays at concerts all over the world, so she doesn't have much time to come here,' he said defensively. 'But when she and Uncle Greg——' He broke off, his eyes widening as if he had just remembered the reason for Cori being there. His look of relief when Ellen appeared in the doorway would have been comical under other circumstances.

'Supper's ready, Bobby,' the housekeeper said comfortably, giving Cori a beaming smile. 'Boss won't be long now, then you can eat too.'

Cori sat perfectly still for long moments after the woman and child had gone from the room. So Bobby had expected his mother to marry Greg! Her mind sought for memories of the famed pianist, coming up with the picture of a startlingly attractive woman whose cameo-perfect features and dark hair drawn back from her face gave a strong impression of tranquillity. A woman, Cori realised suddenly, who would appeal to a man of Greg Mason's calibre. Feminine, yet sure of herself as a person in her own right. Why, then, had he not married her and solved all his problems with one stroke? Married to the mother of his nephew, there would be no need for custody suits or a wife he cared nothing about.

'Why so serious?' Greg's voice cut across her thoughts, making her start and look quickly up to the doorway where he stood in a stark black outfit relieved only by the lighter hue of his skin and flash of white teeth as he went to the bar and poured himself a drink. With his back to her, his hips looked even narrower, his legs longer, in the close-fitting slacks.

'I was wondering why you hadn't married Bobby's mother,' she returned honestly, noting with faint irritation the tightening of his broad shoulders.

'Oh?' he replied laconically, coming across to sit where Bobby had been moments before, leaning forward to place his elbows on his knees, the whisky glass held loosely in both hands.

Cori averted her eyes from the close-fitting vee of his collarless black shirt where midnight-dark hairs curled up towards the powerful shaft of his throat. 'It would have solved a lot of problems for you.'

'It could have,' he agreed evenly after an imperceptible pause. 'But then again it could have caused more. Marisa isn't the type to tie herself down to a remote ranch away from her—public.'

'She's a great pianist. It wouldn't be fair——'

'So my brother thought,' he interrupted drily, rising in one movement when Ellen said from the doorway:

'Supper's ready, Greg. Should I bring it to the table?'

'Yes, thanks, Ellen, we'll be right there.'

Greg's hand came down to encircle Cori's and draw her to her feet. At the contact of his warm dry skin against her own, she told herself that he was obviously putting up the front of being a genuine newly wed husband in front of the housekeeper, and suddenly a shaft of pain re-lit the dull fire of her headache as she went with Greg to the dining room across the hall. How much more genuine would his caressing touch have been if it was Marisa Mason he was leading to the round table overlooking the darkening view beyond the windows? A far less perceptive eye than Cori's would have known that he had not denied the wish to marry Marisa ... only that her public commitments precluded a union between them.

The meal Ellen had prepared was adequate, if uninspiring. Cold beef slices were warmed only slightly with a thin-textured gravy, which also covered the piled mashed potatoes and canned green beans on the plates. A redeeming feature of Ellen's culinary art was the expertly baked dessert of blueberry pie topped with ice cream, followed by well-made coffee and a liqueur Greg brought from the living-room bar.

It was the quietest meal Cori had ever had, and she was startled when Greg said in a harsh voice:

'Does it bother you?'

'What?' Her eyes, quickly alert, met the glittering darkness of his.

'The scar,' he said, raising his head with a jerk as if to indicate the broad white line receding into his hairline.

'Oh.' Embarrassment flooded Cori when she realised she had been staring for several moments at the blemish near his temple, knowing that her wonder as to its cause must have been clearly visible to his eyes. 'Of course not—why should it bother me? As a matter of fact,' she injected a note of lightly enquiring humour into her voice, 'it makes you look very mysterious—as if you'd fought a duel over a beautiful lady.'

His smile was a tautly dry affair that didn't reach his eyes. 'Nothing as romantic as that, I'm afraid. I—tangled with a bear a few years ago.'

Cori's breath drew in sharply as her eyes went from his to the almost dark landscape without. 'Do—do bears live in the hills out there?'

'Bears, and coyotes, and mountain lions—to name a few,' he answered with deceptive casualness. 'But you've no need to worry if you stick close to the ranch buildings. It's only when there's an unusually severe winter that they'll venture near the ranch. When they're desperate for food.'

She shuddered, looking again at the white scar. 'Was that why——? I mean, was the bear——?'

'No. I was on a hunting trip when I ran into this particular bear,' he said in a flat tone that precluded further questioning. His eyes softened slightly as he looked across the table at her pale face and dark-circled eyes. 'Why don't you go to bed and I'll bring something to help that headache?'

Her startled look brought a dry chuckle. 'Don't worry, I won't stay any longer than necessary. I hadn't planned on breaking our agreement.' Ignoring the pale colour that now tinged her cheeks, he went on soberly: 'I realise today's been a strain on you, but I think we can assume the worst is over now.' His eyes met hers. 'You seem to have broken the ice with Bobby already. He's needed a woman about the house.'

'And you haven't?' The words slipped out before Cori could prevent them, and she saw his expression close again.

'I've managed,' was all he said as he rose and came round to pull out her chair. 'Get into bed and I'll be along in a few minutes.'

To Ellen, coming to the doorway at that moment to collect the dishes, it must have seemed as if they were a genuinely loving couple anxious to be alone on their wedding night, and she beamed as Cori passed her with flaming cheeks. The housekeeper said something to Greg in her softly slurred native tongue, laughing at his reply in the same language. Although the words were unintelligible to Cori, their import was clear and she half fled along the passage to the master suite, wondering at Greg's ability to act as if this was a normal marriage. Certainly his performance far surpassed her own.

She was sitting in the tub chair by the window when he came some twenty minutes later. The soft white silk of her robe completely covered the long matching nightdress Doreen had insisted was perfect for a bride's wedding night, and Cori, lost in the painful throes of a pounding headache, had put them on automatically. In the same way, she had pulled back from the acres-wide bed on the point of getting into its inviting softness. For all his carefully controlled self-possession, she knew that the sight of another woman in the bridal bed Greg had envisaged for the one of his choice would be hurtful in the extreme.

She answered his quiet tap with a nervous 'Come in' and his brows rose when he saw her in the chair. One long brown hand circled a glass of milk from which heat rose in a curling vapour, and from the other he produced two white pills as he bent over her.

'You're not in bed?'

'No, I—I thought I'd—sit up for a while.'

'Headache worse?' he enquired with little change in his tone to indicate sympathy, but she sensed it there nonetheless. When she nodded, inexplicably blinking back tears, he said: 'Here, take these. They'll help with the head and also make you sleep better.'

She took the pills from his hand and swallowed them trustingly with some of the soothingly warm milk, not noticing that he had gone behind her chair until she felt his supple hands part her long hair and lie with an almost caressing touch on the nape of her neck.

'Relax,' he said when he felt her stiffen, and she did just that remarkably quickly when his fingers began to massage her neck gently, his thumbs finding the trigger points of her pain and rubbing with increasing pressure until she was aware only of the soothing touch that eased the firepoints of her headache away.

She put the half empty milk glass down on the small round table next to the chair and felt drowsiness overcome her. The pills—or the persistent dry warmth of his hands? It didn't seem to matter either way. The thought uppermost in her mind as her head drooped lower was that the woman who had rejected this man must be a fool. To the one he loved, he could be everything . . .

Her eyes flew open when she felt his fingers unfastening

the tiny buttons on her robe and sliding it from her shoulders.

'Don't worry,' he said softly as he lifted her without effort into the smoothly muscled protection of his arms to carry her to the wide bed. 'I'll leave as soon as I've tucked you in.'

He held her with one arm and pulled back the covers before laying her gently down between the cool satiny sheets, covering her to the neck with the remaining blankets.

'I ... didn't want you to ... see me here,' she murmured sleepily, forcing her lids open to focus her eyes on his face. 'I'm not ... the one you ...'

The sudden blaze in his black eyes might have been prompted by tenderness for herself, or the sparked memory of the woman he had hoped to lie here with, but Cori could fight against sleep no longer and her lashes swept down to her cheeks and stayed there ...

CHAPTER FOUR

THE sun was well up over the Ridge behind the house when Cori woke the next morning and looked round in startled amazement until she remembered where she was and why she was there. The sharply differentiated sounds of birds came from outside the lightly curtained windows, somehow conveying the impression that they had been up and about for hours.

She groped for and found her watch, gasping when she deciphered that it was nine o'clock. There was silence from the rest of the house and she sensed that, like the birds, Greg had been up for hours.

Throwing the covers back, she crossed to the window and blinked when bright light flooded the room as she drew the white mesh curtains aside. The view of mountains and valley seemed different again this morning, sun touching the dark green pines with a misty white glow and lightening the distant peaks to a more shimmering shade of blue. Clearly visible now was the snow topping them with frosty coolness. The river meandered in a solid wide band of frothy silver to meet with a large lake situated far down the valley—the lake Greg had said was too far away for swimming. It was probably too cold anyway, with all those mountains around, and that thought led her to wonder if the pool beside the house was heated.

Leaving that aside as something to discover later, Cori took a quick shower and dressed in clothes she deemed correct for ranch life—slim-fitting blue jeans and white long-sleeved polo-necked sweater in fine wool. She slid her feet into comfortable low-heeled shoes, and as an afterthought tied back her long hair with a blue cotton bandana.

Once through the outer door to the master suite Cori heard sounds of movement from behind the swing doors into the kitchen and she headed for them, her eyes widening as she walked into the biggest kitchen she had ever seen. Painted cabinets in two-tone cinnamon and sand lined the walls and surrounded wide, low-set windows. except for a corner just inside the door to the dining room—this had been set aside as a dining nook with padded leather bench seats stretching along either side of a light coloured formica-topped table. A lavish hand had provided every appliance a cook could need, and the hum of a washing machine came from a small room off the kitchen.

It was from this room that Ellen came, her face breaking out in a shy smile of welcome when she saw Cori.

'Oh, you're up! Boss said to leave you be till you woke yourself, you're pretty tired.' Ellen's smile broadened and her dark eyes were pigeon-bright on Cori's as she added gleefully: 'That Greg's a strong man, eh? Have lots of sons, that one!'

Cori stared uncomprehendingly at the housekeeper for a moment, then understanding dawned and colour dyed her cheeks a brilliant scarlet. Of course—Ellen must have imagined a night devoted to lovemaking by her beloved boss and his new wife!

'Er ... where *is* Greg?' she asked awkwardly.

Ellen chuckled and crossed to a large-sized percolator, reaching for a thick but capacious mug from a long line of hooks under a cupboard.

'Nothing makes any difference to Greg, not even a new wife. He went out same time as always, just after seven. Guess you didn't wake up when he got up.'

'No ... no, I didn't,' Cori answered truthfully. 'And Bobby—is he around?'

'He's at school,' said Ellen, handing Cori the steaming mug. 'Cream and sugar in the dining room. While you drink that, I'll make you some breakfast.'

'At school?' Cori echoed, grasping the mug without thinking. 'But I thought—didn't the teacher leave?'

Ellen snorted derisively. 'That one! Sure, she left, and nobody was sorry to see her go ... scared of her own shadow, she was. Always screaming after Greg that she could hear bears and wolves and goodness knows what else in the hills. Greg was more happy than anybody when he took her away in the plane.'

'Did she live in the house?' Cori asked curiously, perching on the edge of the table and deciding to drink her coffee black.

'No way! That was what she wanted, true enough. but Greg said it wouldn't be right for a single man and woman to live in the house together.' Ellen chuckled again. 'That was just an excuse for him, though. When Mrs Mason comes, they're alone all the time—eat together, go out on the horses together, and no one else is there all the night times when he sits and listens to her play the piano for hours.' Her brown-skinned brow wrinkled in distaste. 'I know Mrs Mason's famous for that, but I get tired of that piano hour after hour, so I go down the hill to visit.' As if realising she had been talking too much, she shook herself and said: 'You go drink your coffee while I make your breakfast.'

At the door into the dining room Cori turned back to ask: 'But who teaches school if the teacher's gone?'

'Jean Raeburn, Mac's wife,' Ellen returned, taking a huge frying pan from under the stove. 'She's no teacher, but she keeps the kids in line and out of their mothers' hair all morning.'

Cori went thoughtfully into the dining room and took the chair where she had sat opposite Greg the night before. Uppermost in her mind was the thought that the ranch children deserved more than being kept out of their mothers' hair for a few hours each day. Greg had originally asked that she come here as their teacher—why couldn't she do just that, even thought her role at Mason's Ridge encompassed far more than a teaching job? She would go mad here in the house while Greg was out all day and Ellen did the housework and cooking. She didn't ride, and after Ellen's scathing remarks about the hapless ex-school-teacher, was determined she would never admit to Greg that the thought of riding a horse scared the living day-lights out of her. Pride, and the knowledge that Marisa Mason went riding with Greg while she was here, stiffened her resolve to master her fear—one day.

She gazed out over the spreading country beneath the window as her thoughts dwelt on Marisa ... it was only too easy to picture the cosy scene in the living room where the beautifully composed woman played to an appreciative Greg. But if he appreciated her so much, why hadn't he married her and solved all his problems at one stroke? Could it really be because, as he had hinted last night, she would never give up her obligation to her 'public'? What about her obligation to her son?

Cori started when Ellen came in and placed a hearty breakfast plate of ham thickly sliced, two eggs and hashed brown potatoes fried to golden crispness in front of her.

'Ellen, I just have toast and coffee for breakfast,' she protested, only to be overruled by the Indian woman's im-perious gesture towards the plate.

'Everybody says that when they first come here from the

city,' she declared flatly. 'Then they find their appetite. I'll see to your room while you eat.'

'No!' Cori half started up in her chair, subsiding back into it and forcing a smile when Ellen looked at her in surprise. 'I—I'd like to take care of that part of the house myself, Ellen. You do everything else, so . . .'

'Do as the missus says, Ellen,' Greg's voice came quietly from the hall. and both women turned their heads in that direction, surprised at not having heard him come in. Cori's heart gave an unaccountable flutter when his deceptively lazy frame came into the dining room, his shoulders tautly broad in a beige denim shirt. Dropping into a chair opposite Cori, he smiled up at Ellen's puzzled face, his strong teeth showing white against the bronzed darkness of his skin.

'You could bring me some coffee,' he suggested placatingly, and Ellen seemed mollified as she returned his smile and disappeared into the kitchen. 'Eat your breakfast before it gets cold,' he turned to Cori again, black eyes peculiarly disturbing in their intentness.

At that moment, nothing could have been less appetising than the stack of food on the plate before her, but Cori began to tackle it manfully, acutely conscious of the dark gaze bent on her.

'I—I don't usually sleep this late,' she told him defensively, as if he accused her by his air of having been up and around for hours doing whatever ranchers did early in the day.

'There's no need for you to rise as early as I do,' he shrugged, thanking Ellen with another smile for the coffee she brought to him. Adding sugar to his cup and stirring with deliberate thoroughness, he went on: 'All I ask is that you play the part of being my wife until the custody hearing is over.'

'And then?' she challenged through another mouthful of food. 'Do you think it's right for the boy to be without a woman's influence in his life?'

'No,' he admitted quietly after a short silence. 'But what I can give him is preferable to wandering the face of the earth with his mother.' Dismissing that subject, he looked at Cori's half empty plate. 'When you're finished, I'll take you down below to meet some of the hands and show you the ranch buildings. Hank's given you a terrific advance press notice!'

'Oh, heavens, I hope not! I nearly always find I'm disappointed when I finally meet somebody who's had a great build-up beforehand.' She jumped to her feet, leaving only a little food on her plate. 'Am I all right like this? I haven't any idea how the boss's wife should dress on a ranch.'

His eyes went slowly down over her figure, slender yet showing all her feminine curves in the clinging wool sweater and tight-fitting jeans.

'I doubt if any of them will be disappointed,' he said softly, the eyes that met hers holding a faint gleam in their depths. 'The married ones will think I'm a very lucky guy, and the single men will curse because they didn't see you first.'

Embarrassment made her voice more flippant than she intended. 'Pity they don't know, then, that I'm really still available, isn't it?'

She was unprepared for the force of his reaction when he stood in one lithe movement and captured her wrist in biting fingers.

'While you stay at the ranch, you're not available to anybody else,' he threw out with dry harshness. 'You will not, by word or gesture, let anyone know that this isn't a legitimate marriage. The stakes are too high for me to take any chances.'

'Don't worry, Greg,' she said coldly, tugging her wrist away from his hold. 'I'm not interested in other men, especially rough, tough ranch types. I like my men to have at least a touch of sophistication.' Unbidden, the thought came into her mind that Greg himself was what might be considered rough and tough, but with the overlying veneer of sophistication she had mentioned. 'I—I'll be ready to go with you in a few minutes,' she murmured, making her escape along the corridor to the master suite.

Once there she made her own bed quickly and hesitated
at the entrance to Greg's room, feeling she was intruding on
his privacy as she turned the handle and went in to see the
tumbled array of bedclothes which denoted a restless
night's sleep. Telling herself that Ellen mustn't be allowed
to wonder about the use of separate bedrooms if she
should by chance come in, Cori schooled herself to im-
partiality and re-made the three-quarter-size bed. Suppressing an involuntary surge of interest in the masculine
accoutrements scattered round the room, she closed the
half open door of the closet on its contents of neatly pressed
work and dress clothes. Greg Mason was a man unto himself, one she suspected was far beyond her understanding.

The winding track down to the valley level was made more
attractive by greenery on either side. Shrubs Cori recognised
as growing at the coast were interspersed with others she
had never seen before, and newly settled summer bedding
plants would provide a blazing cascade of colour in a week
or two.

'Who does the gardening?' she asked Greg as they descended, side by side but not touching. 'And where do you
find the plants away out here?'

Sun slanting down from a clear blue sky made narrow
slits of Greg's eyes when he answered in his slow drawl:
'Joseph takes care of everything in that line, as well as
keeping us supplied with vegetables in season. I pick up
whatever he needs in Williams Lake or Vancouver. Once a
week or so either Hank or I fly into Williams Lake for
supplies and to pick up the mail.'

'You mean we have to wait a week for mail?' she asked,
aghast, stopping to shade her eyes with her hand as she
looked up at him.

He gave a dry chuckle, his eyes amused behind half
closed lids. 'Did you imagine a mailman would make daily
deliveries in his little red truck?' The smile was replaced
by another kind of glitter. 'I thought the idea was for you
to get away from—city ties.'

Cori dropped her hand and walked on again. 'I—I just thought it would be nice to hear from Doreen.'

'Your sister?' He shook his head with a hint of impatience. 'No, Cori, it's not your sister you want to hear from, it's your unfaithful lover boy.' Ignoring her hurt gasp, he went on relentlessly: 'The sooner you put him out of your mind the better it'll be for you and everybody else. Who knows,' his voice was tinged with sarcasm, 'in this case, absence just might make the heart grow fonder!'

Stung, Cori threw up at his impassive face: 'At least he *has* a heart!' But the biggest jolt to her consciousness was that she had not, for one moment, given Roger a thought since her arrival here.

'Meaning I haven't, I suppose,' Greg returned, disconcerting her with his sudden chuckle. 'Maybe you're right, at that.'

The conversation was terminated then as they had emerged on to the flatter land where the heart of the ranch was situated. Bordering the river on their left were barns and log-fenced corrals which seemed to stretch forever, while on the right were buildings obviously designed for the human element ... a square frame building which Cori identified as the school ... when a stumbling young voice came through the open door. a smaller structure which Greg told her was the ranch shop, and further on a long, low building.

'That's the bunkhouse for the unmarried men,' he said, taking her elbow to lead her to the schoolhouse. 'Maybe we should start off here.'

Their feet sounded loud on the plain wooden floor, and the reciting young voice faltered to a stop as they paused inside the door. Cori looked round the room interestedly, seeing the individual school desks spaced in wide rows facing a large blackboard and dark wood table, behind which sat a red-haired, slenderly-boned woman. She rose, and at a gesture from her hand the boy who had been reciting sat down. Greg urged Cori forward and the next few minutes were a daze as she was first introduced to

Jean Raeburn and then to the class of widely aged children,
whose eyes surveyed her with unabashed curiosity—eyes
that ranged in colour from the nut brown of Indian children
to the pale China blue of European stock. Only Bobby's
head remained lowered as if he felt embarrassed at the
presence of his uncle and new aunt. His lips remained
stubbornly closed when the other children chorused, under
Jean's direction, a welcome to the new Mrs Mason.

'All right, children, you can have a ten-minute recess
now,' Jean Raeburn called, and smiled ruefully at the re-
sultant scrabble to reach the sunshine outside. Turning to
Cori, who noticed that at closer range the older woman's
fair skin was sprinkled attractively with freckles, she said:

'I'm really pleased to meet you, Cori—we all thought
Greg would never find himself a wife.' Turning to Greg,
she added accusingly: 'I thought you went to find a
teacher, not a wife!—beautiful though she is.'

Cori opened her mouth to tell the russet-haired woman
that she was a teacher, but Greg's grip on her elbow warned
her not to.

'I've found a qualified teacher for September,' he said
smoothly. 'Her husband's had a lot of ranch experience in
the south, so it should work out pretty well all round.'

Jean made a rueful face. 'September's a long way off. I
know there's only a few weeks left before summer vacation,
but these kids need someone who can teach, not just watch
over them.'

'But I——'

Greg interrupted Cori's involuntary offering of her ser-
vices by saying: 'Do the best you can, Jean. Maybe we can
let them out a little early for this year.'

Outside the schoolhouse Cori turned to him indignantly.
'Greg, *I'm* a teacher—why can't I take over from Jean?'

He said nothing for a few paces, then looked so fierce
that Cori wished she hadn't brought the subject up at all.

'My wife doesn't teach school,' he bit off curtly, and
Cori wasn't sure if he had emphasised the 'my' or 'wife'—
perhaps both, she thought resentfully.

'Oh, don't be so ridiculously old-fashioned!' she snapped. 'What do you expect me to do?—sit up on the hill polishing my nails?'

Almost casually, he slid his fingers down over her forearm and clasped her hand, lifting it to inspect the pink well-kept curve of her nails. The abrasive contact of his fingers on the light wool of her sweater caused a tremor along her nerve ends and she pulled her arm away.

The pause before he walked on again was so brief as to seem unnoticeable. 'These are our prize bulls,' he said evenly when she caught up with him. 'We're experimenting with European stock to see if they'll hold up under our harder winters here.'

Cori scarcely saw the wicked-looking bulls who came over to snort indignantly at the fence, except to note that the enclosure was firmly secured against escape. Strangely, the sight of gleaming flanks on the stable horses further down disturbed her much more than the aggressive pawings of the bulls, and her hands tied themselves into knots when Greg said casually:

'I'll have to teach you to ride. It's a necessity in this country.'

Fear made her voice sharp. 'It's hardly worth the trouble, is it? I won't be here long enough to make use of the lessons.'

His jaw grew taut, but he was saved from replying by the appearance of Hank and two other men who came from one of the barns.

Hank looked incredibly handsome as he swept off his wide-brimmed hat at sight of Cori, his fair-skinned face overlaid with a light tan that emphasised the dark blue of his eyes, the whiteness of perfectly spaced teeth. The blue denim of his shirt and work trousers did little to detract from his attractiveness, and Cori gave him a warm smile to match his.

'Well, the blushing bride looking over the property?' he joked, but the open admiration in his eyes made Cori's shift to the men beside him. She felt Greg's hand on her elbow again.

'This is Mitch, Cori,' he introduced the fractionally taller of the two. 'And Lefty—he cooks for the boys in the bunkhouse.'

Both men pumped her hand with shy roughness, the broad-set Mitch muttering something she didn't hear and Lefty, the bow-legged cook, coming across only too clearly

''Bout time Greg took a wife,' he pronounced, his eyes almost closed in the leathery wrinkles surrounding them. 'He's a great feller, but I won't be sorry to see you soften him up a bit. A man gets ornery and cantankerous without a woman beside him.'

'Like you, Lefty?' Hank put in with a laugh, dodging the blow which the elderly cook aimed at him.

The other men seemed either to be away from the ranch or working in the distant corrals, and Greg took her to examine the machine sheds which contained, so he told her, reapers and balers, tractors and seeders, and a host of other equipment with names unfamiliar to Cori's city ears.

Joseph Clearwater, the small-boned Indian man who tended the large area set aside for vegetables, seemed pleased when Cori asked the reason for the steel mesh fence surrounding the plot.

'That's for the deer,' he explained, his dark eyes twinkling in a smile-creased face. 'They come from the hills and eat all my new plants if they can.'

He took them into a long greenhouse at one side of the enclosure, telling Cori that he started all his vegetables from seed there. And not only vegetables, she noted with an appreciative gasp.

'Joseph, these plants are beautiful!' she breathed as they wandered down between the slatted shelves and came upon a section devoted to flowering house plants. The pale lilac of lantanas blended with the vivid display of geraniums in every colour from lightest pink to brilliant scarlet and begonias vied with the gentle-hued orchid-like plants at the furthest end of the greenhouse, and it was one of these that Joseph lifted to offer Cori.

'You will take this?' he asked, holding out the pot of pale yellow orchids, the outer petals a delicate shade of lilac. 'Just like you—young and fresh, like spring.'

'Oh, Joseph, I——' About to refuse the beautiful plant, Cori glanced up at Greg and saw his faint nod and warning frown, so she amended her words to: 'It's lovely, Joseph. Thank you.'

Greg glanced at his watch as they came out of the greenhouse. 'We'd better leave the rest till another time, Ellen will have lunch ready. There's not a lot more to see anyway.' He pointed to a group of neatly kept bungalows clustered at the river's edge. 'The wives will probably ask you down for coffee in a day or two.'

From that, Cori surmised that she would have to wait for an invitation to visit the attractive-looking homes of his employees, and she appreciated his wish to preserve their privacy.

The schoolhouse was deserted when they passed it on their way back, and Cori now noticed a small cottage set apart from it. Made of varnished logs, its miniature porch lent an air of peaceful calm to it.

'Oh, that's sweet,' she said admiringly, then glanced up to meet Greg's puzzled eyes. 'Is that where I'd have lived if I'd come as the teacher?'

He hesitated. 'Yes. It sounds as if you'd have preferred that to the house.'

'The house is beautiful,' she assured him hastily, sensing his defensiveness about his dream home on the hill. 'But— oh, I don't know,' she went on with unconscious wistfulness as they started the climb up to the main house. 'It must be wonderful to have a place to call your own, where there's only yourself to please.'

'Without even a husband?' he asked drily.

'Yes.' Her tone held a touch of defiance. 'All my life I've had to fall in with what other people wanted to do—first my parents, and then when they retired, Doreen and Howard. Just for once it would be nice to choose for myself where, when and what I'd eat, when I'd go to bed, when I'd get up.' She gave a short, breathless laugh, partly from the steepness of the climb but mostly because she was sure this self-sufficient rancher would scoff at her feelings. And how could she expect otherwise? He had told her he was out riding the range sometimes for weeks at a time doing whatever he did to the cattle, so the ranch must seem like the hub of civilisation to him when he returned to it. Thinking of that, she was surprised when he said:

'I know how you feel,' thoughtfully. 'I have a cabin a couple of miles from here ... I go up there alone sometimes, sometimes with Bobby.'

The look she threw up encompassed the bronzed leanness of his face, the veiled expression in his half-closed eyes. 'You care a lot about Bobby, don't you?' she said softly.

His shoulders remained straight, but there was a shrug in his voice as he said: 'I have a responsibility to him.'

'That's all?' she asked, her breath heavy as they breasted the rise and faced the house, stopping as if by mutual consent to admire its clear-cut lines. 'Isn't there one person in the world you love, Greg?' she turned impulsively to say, and was repelled by the sardonic glitter that immediately sprang to his eyes.

'Love is an overrated commodity,' he pronounced shortly, moving on towards the open front door, his boots crunching heavily on the gravel chips of the circular driveway. Turning back when he reached the porch, he added crushingly: 'It's a myth perpetrated by starry-eyed females like you who clothe natural desires in a romantic haze, so that a man doesn't know what's happening to him until it's too late.'

'You've obviously given a lot of thought to controlling *your* natural desires,' she flared back, lifting her head to stare contemptuously into his face. 'Or don't you have any?'

A muscle in his jaw twitched and his eyes grew hard as

they stared back into hers, then down to her shapely lips quivering with anger.

'Oh, yes, I have them all right,' he said, menacingly soft, and before she had time to realise what was happening he had reached out muscular arms to jerk her roughly against him. One hand secured both wrists behind her back—unnecessarily, because she was too shocked to fight him—and the other fastened in her hair above the scarf tying it back, pulling with cruel fingers until her face was raised to his.

In the split second before his head bent, she saw the light film of perspiration on his brow, the stark whiteness of the scar at his black hairline, the steely determination in his gleaming eyes, and her lips parted in disbelief and more than a little fear. She had never felt so helpless or so completely at the mercy of another human being ... a being who could snap the slender column of her body with one squeeze of a steel-clad arm.

No trace of tenderness softened the harsh pressure of his mouth on hers ... there was only a savagely punishing intentness of purpose that cut off her breath until her senses reeled and her body sagged against the granite hardness of his. He released her wrists, seeming to know that they would hang helplessly at her sides, and his hand moved to the small of her back to exert a pressure that crushed her soft outlines to the unyielding dominance of his and left her in no doubt as to the force of his masculinity.

Cori's mind was wiped clean of any former emotional impression as Greg's lips moved in a demandingly persistent way to suddenly draw a response from her that was as basic and primitive as the hills surrounding them. Her hands moved up over his shirt with a volition of their own to grasp the broad firmness of his shoulders before moving up to clasp behind his neck where the hair was short and crisp between her fingers.

Then, as if each of her finger endings had a viper's sting, Greg pushed her away, a flicker in his dark eyes which could have meant that he too had been moved by the kiss .. or that he was triumphant in knowing he had proved his point without doubt. His next words told Cori that the latter was the case.

'Don't misconstrue that as a breach in our agreement,' he said shortly, his breath coming only a little faster than usual. 'Take it as a lesson that it's dangerous in these parts to put a slur on a man's masculinity.'

Before Cori had time to say a word, he had spun away and disappeared into the house. Trembling, her fingers went up to touch the beginning swell on her lips where his mouth had ground against them and anger shook her, bringing acrid tears to her eyes.

At the same time, the sense of helplessness she had felt in his arms assailed her again. She was completely at his mercy in every way .. she couldn't even leave the ranch without his help, and that help would not be forthcoming until he had fulfilled his purpose of gaining custody of his nephew.

The only chance she might have was in persuading Hank Iverson, the good-looking foreman, to take her out when Greg was away one day. Almost before the thought arose, doubts assailed her. Greg was Hank's boss and, in spite of his obvious admiration for her, loyalty to Greg would always come first. Still

She would have to play it by ear and sound out the ground thoroughly before approaching Hank with definite plans. In the meantime, she would make it clear to Greg that she had no intention of making herself a docile slave to his wishes. She intended to teach the ranch children as best she could for as long as she could.

CHAPTER FIVE

THE opportunity to speak to Greg didn't come until that evening. Cori had changed from the brief bikini she had worn all afternoon at the pool—which she had found was heated to a just-right temperature—and was wearing a high-necked dress in pale yellow when she entered the spacious living room and wandered over to the windows.

Streaks of yellow, pink and orange radiated from behind the midnight blue of the far mountains as the sun set, but her thoughts were far removed from the scenery spread out before her. Strangely, they weren't concerned with Greg either, but with Bobby. The headway she felt she had made with him the evening before seemed to have dissipated in the bright light of the lunch table, and he had seemed almost sullen when he answered the remarks she addressed to him. Finally, she had said brightly:

'How about swimming in the pool with me this afternoon, Bobby?'

'I said I'd go to Scott's house,' he muttered in excuse, then looked appealingly at Greg. 'May I leave now, Uncle Greg?'

'Sure, if you've finished your lunch. But be back by five-thirty.'

When the boy had rushed out without looking at Cori, Greg said quietly: 'Give him time to get used to you. I guess the kids have been teasing him about his ... beautiful young aunt.'

Cori's eyes widened. 'Why should they do that?' she asked, not knowing whether she was questioning the fact of the teasing or that the ranch children might find her beautiful. Greg's next words showed that he favoured the latter angle.

'Don't fish for compliments from me, Cori,' he told her abruptly, rising to his feet and seeming to tower over her seated figure. 'You don't need me to tell you about your looks.'

'No, that's right—I don't,' she had thrown back coolly, and now as she waited for him in the living room, she saw again in her mind's eye the clamped tightness of his jaw, the coldness in his eyes. It was only too easy to remember his kiss devoid of tenderness or care, and her own odd reaction to it. But she mustn't antagonise him on that or any score right now. It would be foolish to do that when he held the key to her relief from boredom and the practice of the job she had been trained to do.

'Can I get you a drink?'

Cori spun round, her thoughts shattering into a thousand pieces when she saw Greg, distinguished yet somehow ferocious in a red shirt and charcoal slacks. Red for danger, she reminded herself only half jokingly, but had to admit that the colour lent vibrancy to his dark good looks.

'I—yes, thanks. The same as last night will be fine.'

For a moment she watched him at the small bar, the back of his dark hair brushed to unwilling neatness, his shoulders rippling with smooth muscled confidence as he poured drinks for both of them. Not a man to cross unless you were very, very sure of yourself, Cori thought as she crossed to one corner of the sectional sofa, unconscious of the spring-like effect of her yellow dress against the dark brown upholstery. But then she *was* sure of herself—wasn't she?

'Greg,' she began as soon as he had handed her the frosty long glass and seated himself in the armchair close to her, 'I want to talk to you about the school.'

His frown was immediate and dark. 'I've already told you that my wife doesn't teach school,' he said in a dismissing tone that set her teeth on edge. 'In the normal course of events, you would have more than enough to do in running the ranch house and entertaining our guests, as well as seeing to the welfare of the families who live here.'

Cori was silenced for a moment, digesting this small speech before protesting: 'But it's not the normal course of events, Greg! I can't take over the running of the ranch knowing that in a few months I won't be here any more. As for entertaining guests—how many do you have, apart from Marisa Mason on infrequent visits?'

'There are others who'll expect to be invited here now I have a wife,' he said flatly, his eyes on the golden liquid in his glass. 'People who have entertained me in the past.'

'Oh, Greg,' she whispered, her eyes wide hazel orbs in the muted light from the side lamps illuminating the room.

'You should have taken a proper wife, one you could love and who would love you.'

One eyebrow quirked up in sardonic remembrance. 'I thought we'd been through the love business earlier today and settled it once and for all.'

Colour swept across her face at his reminder of those agonising few minutes on the porch. The half amused gleam in his eyes told her that he, too, remembered the response he had elicited from her, thus proving his point that romantic love was unnecessary in the satisfying of 'natural desires'. In spite of the heated state of her face, Cori shivered. Such cold-blooded logic could only appeal to a man of Greg Mason's type—arrogant, aggressive, expecting no tenderness and giving none. Pity filled her for any woman who fell in love with him.

Nothing more was said that evening about Cori taking on the education of the ranch youngsters, and she filled the ensuing days with a meaningless round of desultory housekeeping in the master suite and long afternoons spent in or beside the pool in a brief bikini which exposed most of her skin to the penetrating rays of a hot sun and turned it to honey gold.

Bobby always disappeared as soon after lunch as he could, and Greg took to paper work in his study across the hall as soon as dinner was over, excusing himself on the grounds that necessary accounts work had been neglected during his absence in Vancouver. Some evenings, Cori went to bed without even saying goodnight to him ... and he seemed to lose himself completely in whatever he happened to be doing, whether physical or mental. Achingly, she longed for some kind of occupation that would absorb her own mental and physical capacities.

Ten days after her arrival at the ranch, Greg for once left before Bobby when lunch was over. The day was more than usually warm, and the sun glinted temptingly off the blue pool. Almost as a last effort, Cori suggested: 'Why don't you bring your friends up for a dip in the pool, Bobby?'

A flash of interest lit his eyes momentarily, and then he shook his head. 'Uncle Greg said we couldn't use the pool unless he was here to look after us.'

'Oh. Well, I'm sure he meant you couldn't unless there was a grown-up to supervise you. I'm a grown-up, and I can swim pretty well.' As added incentive. she added: 'I'd appreciate a little company—it gets lonely swimming all by myself.'

Reluctantly, Bobby said: 'Uncle Greg wouldn't like it if we bothered you.'

'You leave Uncle Greg to me,' she returned confidently, more concerned about making a point of contact with Bobby than with Greg's possible displeasure. 'Go down and collect your friends, and we'll have some fun.'

Bobby gave an uncharacteristic whoop of joy and charged off to the lower regions of the ranch complex while Cori, happier than she had been since her coming, changed into a less brief bikini. Eyeing herself critically in the full-length mirror in her bedroom, she wished she had brought a more conservative outfit, but reflected that the youngsters probably wouldn't notice the amount of golden flesh revealed by the hip-hugging floral briefs and reasonably adequate bra top.

A few minutes later she blinked as every child who went to the ranch school came trooping from the front of the house. Of course! In a place as isolated as Mason's Ridge, no one could be left out. Boys outnumbered the girls ten to four, but no concessions on those grounds were expected or given. After their initial shyness with her wore off, they joined wholeheartedly in the races Cori organised by size rather than age, and soon the lithe copper bodies of native Indian children mingled with their paler counterparts to churn up the sparkling water as they raced from side to side.

Ellen appeared halfway through the afternoon, beaming as she carried a tray laden with lemonade and the cookies she had just baked. 'Come and help me with this, Jason,' she called to the gentle-mannered Indian boy who was the oldest of the group and who had been helping Cori with the younger children. Obediently he came, the soft blackness of his hair falling over his brow and almost obscuring the liquid darkness of his eyes.

While they sat in a companionable huddle eating and drinking, Cori quizzed them unobtrusively about their school work and found that their answers stirred to a higher pitch her own frustrated longing to do the job she had been trained for. Even her inexperienced eye could see that the fourteen-pupil school was a challenge no natural-born teacher could resist.

Time raced by as Cori organised a primitive game of water polo, restricted as it was to the shallow end of the pool, but it was still earlier than Greg's normal homecoming time when she looked round from where she stood laughing at the pool's edge, her arms poised with the ball above her head, and saw him in the dining room doorway, which was open to the children's clamour. The excited shouts of 'Throw it to me, Mrs Mason!' and 'No, me, Mrs Mason' faded as Cori's eyes locked with the amused gleam in Greg's. Sudden shyness overtook her as his gaze went down to make a slow inspection of her long-legged figure, the golden tan of her skin sparkling with water drops, and she threw the big ball at random into the pool, where the children fell on it with gleeful shouts.

Bobby, however, detached himself from the others and swam to the side of the pool to look up into the tall man's face as he crossed the patio slowly at right angles to Cori. Damp patches darkened the blue denim of his open-necked shirt, and pale-coloured dust streaked his face.

'Why don't you come in, Uncle Greg?' Bobby pleaded eagerly. 'You never come in the pool now,' he added accusingly.

'Some of us have to work for a living,' Greg tossed down a smile to the anxious face. 'But as I've taken the rest of this afternoon off, maybe I will come in.'

The edges of his smile remained when he walked round to Cori's side. 'I wondered who the Pied Piper of Mason's

Ridge was ... I couldn't see a child above five years old down below.'

'I hope you don't mind that I asked them up to swim,' Cori returned politely, the odd sense of embarrassment keeping her eyes averted from his.

'Mind? Why should I mind if you don't? It's your privacy that's being invaded.'

She cast a quick look, then at his brows lifted in a genuinely puzzled arc. 'A person can only take so much privacy, I find,' she remarked with a trace of tartness. 'I've enjoyed this afternoon more than any since—for a long time,' she amended diplomatically.

'You find it lonely here?' he asked, ludicrously at that moment, for he had to raise his voice several notches to overcome the screams from the pool beside them.

'Isn't any prisoner lonely at times?' she taunted, seeing his look of shocked surprise as she left to walk round the pool's edge to dive cleanly into the deep end.

When she surfaced, Greg had gone and she wondered fleetingly if she had offended him with her remark, then mentally shrugged as she rejoined the children. What was she but a prisoner when she couldn't leave the perimeter of Mason's Ridge of her own free will? Even the other wives seemed to be shunning her ... but whether that was Greg's doing or theirs she had no way of knowing.

A few minutes later, however, when she looked up it was to see Greg poised at the deep end of the pool, close to where she herself had dived in, his expression more one of thoughtfulness than anger. In black swimming trunks, his body seemed more perfectly proportioned than ever. Wide bronzed shoulders above a capacious chest covered lightly with dark hair led to tapered hips and flat, muscled stomach, ending in legs that were long and powerful.

His dive into the water was knife-like, and Cori was still faintly breathless with her unbidden thoughts of admiration for his masculine grace when he surfaced close by and was fallen on by the delighted youngsters. Tremulously, she wondered what it would be like to be loved by a man like

Greg Mason. How would she have felt if the husband who now played with the children in the pool was her husband in every sense of the word?

The strange sensations evoked by this unplanned meditation spread a nervous reaction akin to panic through her body, and she pushed out to the deep end, turning to float on her back back while the excited squeals of the youngsters reverberated round her head. Roger was the only reality in her love life, not Greg Mason with his masterful, uncompromising ways that precluded love in a romantic form. It was all an animalistic ritual to him ... a chemical reaction where nothing above the physical was asked, nothing above the physical given ...

Seconds later she was struggling for the physical reassurance of the shoulders she had admired only minutes before. Strong fingers had encircled her ankles and pulled her down under the water, shocked surprise making it easy for the water to fill her nose and mouth and leave her gasping as she came up for air clutching frantically at Greg's cool hard flesh. Sounds faded from her consciousness, and she knew only the comforting strength of Greg's arms encompassing her, pulling her, lifting her from the water and then laying her on a full-length lounge chair close to the pool.

'Cori? Cori, are you all right?'

Water-spiked lashes opened over eyes that sparked fury in their hazel depths. 'You are an idiot, Greg Mason,' Cori enunciated clearly, ignoring the concern his voice had conveyed. 'Now all these ... children will be ... following your example and ... doing a good job of drowning each other!'

Greg looked assessingly at her for a long moment, then rose from his kneeling position beside her to go to the children, who were already climbing out of the pool, awe written on their faces.

'You've just seen a good example of what not to do in a pool,' he said grimly. 'If I ever see any of you try a foolish thing like that, I'll tan your hide myself, okay?' No one

seemed capable of answering him. 'All right, dry your-
selves off and go on home. Your mothers will have supper
ready.'

Cori forced a smile to her lips as the youngsters gave
themselves a perfunctory rub down with their towels and
filed past her. The afternoon that had started so promisingly
seemed to have ended like a fizzled-out balloon, but Cori
nevertheless sensed a shy acceptance of her in their scheme
of things as they smiled on their way out.

When the last of them had gone and Greg had sent
Bobby to change for supper, she murmured antagonisti-
cally: 'And who tans *your* hide for doing such a foolish
thing?'

Greg sat on the edge of her chair and for one unbelievable
moment looked like one of the chastened youngsters, his
hair smoothed wetly back on his head, unusually long
black eyelashes clustered in moist points above penitent
dark eyes.

'I guess you should have that privilege,' he said with
surprising candour, although his face then assumed its
normal expression of detached authority. 'I'm sorry, Cori. I
didn't realise you'd be so caught up in your thoughts that
you wouldn't know I was around.' A faint bitterness edged
his voice, and Cori wondered guiltily what he would think
if he knew the contents of her mind at that time. She had
been wondering what it would be like if he was really her
husband. The reality of his overpoweringly masculine closeness to her now made her voice flippant.

'Well, as I don't carry my special whip for tanning hides
around in my bikini, I'll let it go this time,' she said lightly,
swinging her feet to the concrete. 'Race you to the shower!'

The expression of total surprise on his face followed her
as she sped through the dining room and along the passage,
and a wave of compassion washed over her. There had been
altogether too little fun in Greg Mason's life, that much
was obvious, and although she herself was not destined to
be the one to bring that quality to his life, she sincerely
hoped that one day he would give his heart to the special

woman who could charm him occasionally from his normal sombre state.

'You seemed to get on well with the kids today,' Greg remarked casually at dinner that night. 'I was thinking that —maybe you would like to teach them for the rest of the school year.'

'But of course I would!' Cori returned smartly, annoyed that he should make it sound as if the suggestion was his but unable to keep the starry sparkle from her eyes. 'It's what I want more than anything else at this moment.'

He looked at her quizzically. 'You're very easily pleased —or is it a case of any port in a storm of loneliness?'

Cori flushed, but admitted frankly: 'That's part of it. I'm not used to filling idle hours until my lord and master comes home,' sarcastically. 'And finding that when he does, he's shut up in his office most of the evening.' She stopped, biting the soft part of her lower lip, knowing her words sounded like a complaint of his neglect.

'Would you prefer it if I spent more time with you?'

Confusion clouded her eyes as they met his level stare. Visions of a blissfully happy twosome close together on the couch, reading or listening to music on the stereo set, faded abruptly in the light of reality. The distance between them could never be bridged by more hours of togetherness.

'No ... no, I'll be quite happy being with the children all day. By the way,' she added hurriedly, 'I think they should put in a normal school day, they've missed so much lately. Do you think their mothers would mind?'

His shoulders lifted in a careless shrug that indicated he had withdrawn again. 'You're the teacher. You'll decide the hours. Anyway,' he stood and lifted his coffee cup, obviously about to depart for the office again, 'you'll find out more tomorrow night. The women have been planning a party for us—they wanted to do it last Saturday, but I suggested they wait till you were more settled at the ranch.'

'Or until I was more used to playing my role of boss's

wife?' she queried waspishly, irritated because he had not at least told her the reason for the ranch women's unfriendliness.

'Maybe,' he conceded quietly. 'If it's any comfort to you, it's no easier for me than it is for you.'

His words lingered in the air after he had gone, and she sat staring through the windows at the twilit night. Apart from a few odd moments, she had never given much thought to his side of their bargain. Now she reflected thoughtfully that it must be infinitely harder for him, mixing every day with people he had known for years, parrying the inevitable ribald jokes a newly married man was subjected to. The only adult Cori had had dealings with was Ellen, and there had been no real need to convince the housekeeper about the realness of their marriage.

Just how well Greg was capable of playing his part was evidenced the following night when, in the schoolhouse bare of desks and decorated with flowers and paper streamers, he stood on the small dais with an arm round Cori's waist and made a short speech of introduction.

'My wife . . .' he paused as if expecting the whistles and comments that came from the younger men, '. . .wanted to meet you all long before now, but I was selfish enough to want to keep her to myself for a while.' His smile remained while a voice came from the back:

'Why would you want to do that, Greg?'

'If you don't know, Jim, maybe you and I should have a little talk tomorrow morning.'

When the laughter had died down again, Greg looked down into Cori's pink-flushed face and said: 'Cori's a newly qualified teacher, and although I didn't want to lose her to the kids this soon, it seems she's worried that they've lost quite a lot of their education lately and she'd like to teach them for the rest of the school year.'

The applause that came from both men and women showed their appreciation and concern for their children, and Cori was relieved to see that the red-haired Jean Raeburn clapped as enthusiastically as anyone.

Hank had been waiting at the side, ready to put a record on the portable stereo, and at a nod from Greg his arm dropped and lively music filled the air. A fresh-faced young hand, tall and rugged as most of the men seemed to be, came to ask Cori to dance. An unaccountable flutter of panic swept over her as Greg removed his arm from her waist, and she realised suddenly that she had been leaning heavily against his side for support. His eyes followed her as the younger man swept her on to the bare wood floor, and she drew a strange kind of comfort from his barely perceptible nod. Unbidden, the memory of their wedding came into her mind. Then, as now, the dark sureness of his gaze supported her—she had felt that without the magnetic pull of those eyes drawing her down the aisle she would have fled in panic from the church.

One pair of stalwart arms followed another until Cori felt she must have danced with every man on the ranch twice, but a respite came with the supper break, when she had a chance to talk to the wives who had prepared the food which strained the capacity of a large trestle table at one side of the room.

'You must all have worked like beavers,' she said admiringly to the women clustered round her at the table, their names and faces a jumble in her mind. 'I'm—*Greg* and I are very grateful for your thoughtfulness.'

'It was our pleasure,' smiled a matronly-looking blonde woman, her eyes going over Cori's simple but well-cut floral dress. 'I can see now why Greg swept you off your feet in Vancouver and wanted to keep you hidden away up there at the house! We'll all have to keep our husbands chained to the doorpost with you around!'

Cori laughed in embarrassment, but was saved from replying by Jean Raeburn's sarcastic comment.

'Why would Cori be interested in your Tom when she's married to Greg Mason? He's a package I wouldn't have minded finding under *my* Christmas tree once upon a time!' More seriously, she turned to Cori and said: 'I'm so relieved to know that you'll be taking over the school, Cori. Greg kept it very dark that you were a teacher.'

Cori smiled awkwardly. 'Well, I think he just didn't want me to work—so soon after being married, I mean.'

'They're all like that to begin with, honey,' a laconic drawl came from a tall and dark slender woman at the rear, 'but just wait a year or two until the kids start coming. Then you won't stand a chance against poker with the boys in the bunkhouse.'

'Hush up, Sherry,' the blonde woman said irritably. 'Just because you can't keep Bob home at night it doesn't mean Greg——'

'I'm going to steal my wife away for a while and dance with her for the first time . . . tonight,' Greg put in smoothly from behind Cori, and she wondered if anyone else had noticed the slight pause before his 'tonight'—it wouldn't have done for the other women, especially the dark-haired Sherry, to know that they had never before danced together.

A tremor of misgiving shook Cori as Greg took her in his arms, but after the first tense moments she relaxed and followed his steps effortlessly. His arm tightened round her, drawing her close to the smooth hardness of his body under the light gold of his shirt, and her nostrils were filled with the faint scent of the soap he used, the spicy drift of cologne from his jaw so close to her temple, and the lingering aftermath of the cigar he had smoked before coming down to the schoolhouse. Although she knew it was no more than a gesture of proof to the watchful eyes around them, when his cheek came down to rest against the silky thickness of her hair it felt just right there.

'Would *you* do that?' she murmured, and wished she hadn't spoken, for his head lifted immediately.

'Do what?'

'Leave your wife to play poker with the boys once the kids started coming.'

His eyes flickered over hers, then looked over her head. 'That would depend on the wife, I suppose,' he said at last.

'If you're talking about Sherry's remark—she and Bob are having problems. Problems I don't mean to have in my life.'

'But how can two people be sure?' she persisted, wishing vaguely that he would rest his head against hers again and knowing from his tight-lipped expression that he would not.

'By not looking at each other through a romantic haze at the start,' he said coldly, and seemed relieved that the dance ended at that moment.

But long after the evening's entertainment was over, after they had climbed the hill to the eyrie they shared yet didn't share, Cori was thoughtful. Undressing in the luxurious master bedroom, she wondered again what—or who—had given Greg his antipathy towards romantic love.

Never had time gone so fast for Cori as did the next three weeks—two until the normal end of the school year and an extra week tacked on by mutal consent between Cori and the parents.

Teaching a class of only fourteen children at first sight seemed a teacher's dream, but Cori soon discovered that teaching such a wide age range presented a sizeable problem in itself. Her own inclination was to have the children express themselves verbally on the subjects they were studying, but this was obviously impossible with only two or three in each grade level.

Jason, the gentle-mannered Indian boy who would be eligible to go to secondary school as a boarder in September, worked happily at the assignments she gave him, but the younger children were more of a problem. Easily distracted, they would much rather spend their school hours chattering and giggling among themselves.

At dinner after three days of teaching, Greg noticed the pensive furrow between her brows. 'Something bothering you, Cori?' he asked when Ellen had brought their coffee.

'What? Oh, no . . . well, yes, there is something . . .' Feeling inadequate, she told him what the problem was in as few words as possible and was amazed at his serious consideration of it, seeming not to think her foolish or in-capable at all.

'You could separate the age groups a little more,' he suggested. 'Why don't you use the porch of the teacher's cottage for the older ones who can be trusted to work on their own? It would be a lot easier to keep the younger kids in line if they had your sole attention at least part of the time.'

'Could we do that?' she asked, a sparkle of hope light-ing her eyes.

'I don't see why not,' he shrugged. 'You could try it for a day or two anyway.'

'Greg, you're a genius!' she beamed admiringly. 'Why didn't I think of that?'

'You would have, given time,' he returned drily, getting to his feet and lifting his coffee as he normally did prior to disappearing into the office, but this evening he surprised her by saying: 'Would you like to listen to some music in the living room? I have some of Marisa's records if you'd care to hear them.'

'I—I'd love to. I just adore her playing.'

'Yes, she's . . . talented.'

Cori curled up in the corner of the sofa she had come to consider hers, accepting with a smile the liqueur he placed beside her coffee cup on the table between them. By the time he came back to take the armchair, a generous measure of brandy in his glass, the clear notes of a Chopin waltz filled the room.

Cori was immediately transported to the concert hall in Vancouver where she had sat enraptured while Marisa Mason coaxed notes of pure silver from the piano. Almost, she could see the dark-haired beauty seated at the piano by the window, her slender fingers flashing over the keys. No wonder Greg . . .

Her eyes lifted to his profile, silhouetted in the subdued light from a lamp behind him, surprised to see that his jaw was drawn into a tight line, his mouth compressed to uncompromising hardness, his eyes dark pools of unfathomable emotion. Cori's own emotions were coolly detached as the certainty came to her that Marisa Mason was at the root of Greg's aversion to the idea of romantic love.

Pity unexpectedly swept over her in a wave so strong that she had to draw her eyes away from his face to the impersonal blackness of the wide windows at the far side of the room. First to be thwarted in his love by the fact of Marisa's marriage to his brother, and even after that brother's death knowing that he could never keep Marisa's superb talent hidden away here in the hills. Could it be that the custody suit was Greg's way of ensuring that Marisa would visit the ranch at least occasionally?

'Greg, if you don't mind, I'll go to bed now,' she said hurriedly, rising as the plaintive notes of Beethoven's Moonlight Sonata stole across the room. 'No, don't get up ... I'll see you tomorrow. Goodnight.'

Not waiting for any reply he might make, she went quickly to the door, conscious only of Greg's eyes on her back ... eyes that looked but seemed not to see.

Greg's suggestion about segregating the age groups worked remarkably well and, though the younger children resented her added surveillance at first, they soon accepted the inevitable and buckled down to work.

Jason, who took it upon himself to supervise the older pupils on the cottage porch, was a joy to teach. His bright mind quickly grasped the more advanced work of his grade, and Cori wished she could spend more time with him. But even with the extended school day, she still found herself taking textbooks back to the house to mark in the evening.

On one of those evenings, Greg had come into the living room to pour himself a brandy, frowning when he saw her in her favourite corner of the sofa, books propped on her knee.

'There's another desk you could use in the office,' he suggested casually.

'Won't it bother you if I'm in there too?' Her head twisted round to look up at him. and she was surprised to see a relaxed smile on his firm mouth.

'I'll let you know if it does.'

Yes, you would too, she thought wryly as she followed him across the hall to the panelled study, a room she had spent little time in since her arrival. It was a cosy room, well lit, yet the wall and table lamps seemed to shed a rosy glow of intimate warmth, even over the starkly grey filing cabinets beside Greg's desk. Books lined the wall just inside the door ... a collection Cori had been surprised to find included the latest novels as well as ranching and agricultural tomes.

Greg, who had helped to carry her books, removed several big ledgers from a desk considerably smaller than his own in front of the window.

'Will my cigar bother you?' he asked, indicating the lit cigar in an ashtray as he went to sit behind his desk.

'No ... no, I like it,' she said honestly, knowing that long after she had left Mason's Ridge for good, the lingering aroma of a sweet yet pungent cigar would conjure up Greg in her mind.

The knowledge that from his vantage point behind his desk he could see her without moving his position, whereas she would have to turn her head to see him, bothered her at first and she let her hair hang like a silk curtain beside her face. As she became engrossed in her work, however, her left hand came up to brush the hair back and pinion it over her ear. She was unconscious now of the heavy gold wedding band and diamond circlet engagement ring Greg had placed on her third finger, though at first they had seemed a constant reminder of the falsity they symbolised.

It became a habit for them to work together in the office after that, and a form of comradeship grew between them during those evening hours, although Cori was careful about disturbing him with idle talk when his knitted brow was bent over his papers and ledgers.

One night, however, when she was reading the essay

Jason had handed in that day, a soft exclamation broke from her.

'What is it?'

She cast a guilty glance over her shoulder. 'I'm sorry, Greg. It's this essay of Jason's.'

'Is it that bad?'

'No! It's that good. This boy has real talent, Greg, he could go far.'

'Is it against the rules for me to see it?'

'Well ...' she hesitated, then smiled and rose with the exercise book in her hand. 'I don't think Jason would mind *you* seeing it.'

Her face lit with enthusiasm, she came round the desk to put the book in front of Greg, her hair brushing softly against his cheek as she bent. He sat very still for a long moment before leaning forward to read the neat script, and Cori leaned backwards on the desk beside him as his eyes scanned the pages.

'Well?' she asked impatiently when he at last sat back again.

'It's good,' he admitted slowly. 'It's very good. But, Cori'—he looked up at her with a vaguely worried expression—'don't build this up out of proportion. An ability such as this can be more of a handicap than an asset to a boy like Jason.'

She stared down disbelievingly into his eyes, only half aware that his seated position made him more manageable somehow.

'You mean because he's Indian?'

'Exactly.' He raised an admonishing hand when her cheeks flooded with pink. 'Now don't go jumping to the wrong conclusions! I'm no more prejudiced than you are, but there's more to think about in this case than just that. I've spent a lot of time and effort persuading Jason's family that he could go on to further education, but look at it from their point of view—from Jason's point of view.'

Cori abruptly lost her advantage when he stood and looked down at her. 'So he goes away to school, and then I guess you're thinking of university for him ... but what happens when he comes back, Cori? To a people he no longer has any point of contact with?' His long forefinger tapped the pages on the desk. 'You can see from this that he loves this country, and the old ways of his people—this is where he wants to be, not in some city where there's only concrete for his feet to walk on.'

Cori blinked under the intensity of his gaze. 'But he can help his people by writing ... like this ... about the things that are important to them.'

'I think he can do that better from this background.' Unexpectedly, his hand cupped her chin and lifted it so that her eyes were looking directly into his. 'It's a pity you won't be staying on at the Ridge ... you could have helped him a lot.' He sighed then and dropped his hand. 'It's getting late, Cori. Let's go to bed.'

The easy way he said the last words, as if they were a normal married couple, pointed up the improvement in their relationship and Cori was glad of that, but deeper colour ran up under the honey gold of her tanned cheeks as she turned away to collect her books.

Greg's whole attitude towards the man–woman relationship was diametrically opposed to her own, so why were her pulses fluttering disturbingly as she followed him from the room? Were they proving his point that physical attraction alone was enough between two people?

CHAPTER SIX

'UNCLE Greg, are you taking a fishing rod for Cori?' Bobby shouted from half way down the stairs. The tall man halted at the front door, turning back to meet Cori's eyes as she came from the kitchen carrying a picnic basket.

'If she'd like one, certainly,' said Greg, raising his brows interrogatively at Cori.

'I've never fished, but I'd love to try,' she smiled gaily in keeping with the holiday spirit that had enveloped them all from early that Saturday morning.

Ellen had left the evening before for a two-day visit with her ageing father in the village five miles upriver, and Cori had felt an upsurge of pleasure that morning in preparing breakfast for the three of them, then getting together the picnic lunch to take to the lake. She packed the cold chicken pieces Ellen had left for their supper that night, and took two large steaks from the freezer for the meal she intended to prepare on their return.

'You'll need a hat of some kind,' Greg told her when he came back from the rear of the house with another light-tempered rod, his eyes going over her neatly tied back hair. 'The sun can be pretty fierce out in the middle of the lake.' He himself had substituted a peaked cotton hunting cap of bright red for the wide-brimmed hat he normally wore, and looked ready for a relaxed day's fishing in worn beige cotton drill pants and white tee-shirt.

'I don't have one, but I've been out in the sun a lot lately. so it won't matter.'

'You must have something,' he returned shortly. 'Mine would be too big for you ... don't you have a cap Cori could borrow, Bobby?'

Delighted to be of use to the girl who had come to Mason's Ridge as his unwelcome aunt and more recently had become the most popular teacher the Ridge had known —making him the envy of his fellow pupils—Bobby ran upstairs and came back breathlessly a moment later with a white cap that fitted Cori's small head perfectly.

The jeep was fully loaded when Greg went back into the house as if he had forgotten something, on his return thrusting a wrapped object between the tightly wedged paraphernalia on the back seat beside Bobby. Then at last they were away, Cori scarcely noticing the bumpy ride she had found so objectionable on her arrival at the ranch. Every second the clear sparkling water of the lake drew closer, blue where the sky reflected its colour in the centre, jewel-like green round the edges where firs swept to the shore.

While Greg and Bobby went to take a sleek silver boat from a log-crafted boathouse at the water's edge, Cori investigated the small strip of golden beach. Trees providing shade were interspersed at the perimeter of the sand, but closer to the water unbroken sunshine spilled down from a blue sky. A children's paradise, she thought, gazing out over the rectangular lake to the further shores. Anyone's paradise, she amended silently. The silence was so broad and vast it seemed as if they were the only people left in the world. Or were they the first people in Paradise, she wondered with a wry smile ... had Adam been like Greg, seeing Eve as a means of fulfilling 'natural desires'? Somehow, she felt sure that Eve would have had a word or two to say about that!

'Are you coming fishing, or would you rather stay there and dream?' Greg's voice broke in.

'Oh, fishing by all means,' she called back, and ran hastily across the sand to the small jetty leading from the boathouse, where Greg handed her in to sit beside Bobby on the broad end seat. She was glad there was no motor to disturb the primeval peacefulness, only the steady dip of the oars Greg wielded until they were near the centre of the lake.

Bobby baited his own hook, but Greg attached a small orange-red salmon egg to Cori's and showed her how to send it spinning in an arc across the water before reeling in. Confidence increased with each cast, and Greg soon left her to it while he saw to his own rod.

Not even Bobby spoke, and the silence was so absolute that Cori lapsed into a state between sleep and wakefulness so that when a sharp tug came at the end of her line the rod almost dropped from her hand and she uttered a surprised: 'Oh!'

'Keep your rod up,' Greg commanded tersely, winding in his own line and stowing the rod along the side of the boat. 'Just wind in steadily ... don't adjust the drag.'

Cori looked at him in round-eyed helplessness as these confusing instructions issued from his lips, and he said quietly to Bobby:

'Slide over here nice and easy, Bobby, so I can sit with Cori and bring him in.'

A moment later the transfer had been effected and Bobby watched wide-eyed as Greg's arms encircled Cori, his bronzed hands covering hers on rod and reel.

'That's it—keep it up, like this. Feel him pull?' When she nodded dumbly he went on, excitement underlying his quietly spoken words: 'Keep winding in although he's running ... here he comes now ... that's the boy ... see him, Cori?'

'Yes ... yes, he's *huge*!' Her own voice sparked with excitement as she saw the speckle-backed trout thrashing the water near the boat. 'Oh, Greg, I can't ... you bring him in.' The tension suddenly left her body and she rested against the taut firmness of his, surprised at her own reluctance to leave it when he urged:

'Come on, you can do it ... he's almost to the boat ... here he comes ... there! Isn't he a beauty?'

For a moment the glittering trout hung in the air, seeming enormous to Cori's inexperienced eyes, and she smiled exultantly into Greg's face, inches from her own, seeing the answering flash of white teeth in the grained mahogany of his skin. Then the beautiful fish lay dead at the bottom of the boat, and Cori felt slightly sick as she looked at it.

'Wow! That's a biggie!' said Bobby, his eyes big with admiration. 'You're a good fisherman, Cori.'

'Beginner's luck,' Greg growled, but his smile belied his words as he changed places with Bobby again. Cori was glad when he wrapped the dead fish in paper and stowed it under his seat out of the sun. Already the radiant colours had begun to fade.

Bobby caught a small trout and Greg brought in two weighing slightly less each than hers before they made for shore and lunch. Greg cleaned the fish at the jetty while Cori put out their lunch under a tree.

'Pity we brought food from home,' he remarked regretfully as he came to join her and Bobby on the blanket she had spread on the sand. 'We could have built a fire and cooked the fish.'

Cori shuddered. 'No, thanks. I definitely prefer the chicken.'

'I'll cook them for breakfast tomorrow,' he promised as if bestowing a priceless gift on her. 'There's nothing like fresh lake trout—better in the open, of course, but . . .'

Just before they started to eat Cori discovered that the mysterious last-minute package Greg had stowed in the back seat was a bottle of sparkling white wine, cool from its lake-fresh resting place beneath the jetty.

Sated, they lay drowsily on the blanket until Bobby, near the adults' feet, forced some animation into his voice.

'Should we go fishing again, Uncle Greg?'

'No.' The answer was definite, and Bobby subsided on his back. 'Siesta time now.'

'Aw, Uncle Greg, does that mean you and Cori are going to be kissing and that junk?' the boy persisted in a disgusted voice, raising himself on one elbow to frown at them. 'The feller said . . .'

'It's too hot for kissing and that junk,' Greg said drily, 'whatever the fellers said. Lie down and go to sleep.'

As if setting an example, he pulled his own hat further down over his eyes and slid down from the tree he had been leaning against to lie on his back and close his eyes. Bobby glowered at him for another moment, then assumed an identical position with a heavy sigh.

Within minutes, the regular breathing of man and boy told Cori they were asleep. After brushing a fly from Greg's cheek, she slid down to a prone position beside him and stared up through the dry-looking aspen leaves to the blue sky above. Had he really thought it was too hot for kissing and that junk?

Despite the sleep after lunch, Bobby's eyes were heavy again when they reached home just after six.

'I'd planned he could eat with us tonight,' Cori told Greg in the hall, 'but it doesn't seem as if he'll hold out that long.'

'Just give him something quick. He ate well earlier, so a light supper won't hurt him.'

While Bobby made sporadic inroads into a bowl of soup and crackers, Cori busied herself seasoning the steaks she and Greg were to have and putting potatoes wrapped in foil to bake in the oven. By that time Bobby was almost asleep over his soup bowl, and for the first time she took him upstairs to bed.

She had made a cursory tour of the upper rooms shortly after her arrival, only popping her head briefly round Bobby's door to see the pleasant sloped ceiling room with dormer window overlooking the valley and river. Now she stood aghast and looked at the unmade bed and numerous pieces of clothing strewn round the floor and furniture. It was only too obvious that Ellen's presence was missed in this room at least.

'Oh, Bobby,' she said reproachfully, 'how could you leave your room in a mess like this?' Remembering his tiredness, she moderated her tone slightly. 'You hop into the bath while I make your bed and tidy up a little. Would you like me to run the water for you?'

'Yes, please, Cori.'

Realising from his subdued reply that she had been using her schoolmarm voice on him, she smiled when she told him to bring clean pyjamas to the bathroom next door.

A lump rose in her throat when she went back to the bedroom and saw that he had made a haphazard effort to tidy it while she had been running his bath. Poor Bobby! He needed a mother so much, and Cori wondered at a woman who could leave an adorable son to the bachelor ministrations of his uncle.

Her eye fell on a framed photograph on the bedside table after she had made the bed up neatly, and she lifted it to look more closely. The dark-haired, attractive woman was without doubt Marisa Mason, but the man beside her was a puzzle to Cori. Surely that fair-haired and blue-eyed man could never be Greg's brother? Yet there was a certain similarity in facial contour that could indicate a relationship. She was thoughtful as she picked up the remainder of Bobby's clothes and put them in the hamper provided for them.

Just as she was wondering if she should check on him, Bobby appeared in the doorway, his dark hair ruffled over bright eyes and cheeks reddened by the sun.

'Who are these people in the picture, Bobby?' she asked as she tucked the clothes round his fine-boned figure.

'That's Mommy ... and Daddy,' he answered sleepily, adding accusingly: 'I thought you said you saw Mommy play at a concert.'

'Yes ... yes, I did,' Cori assured him hastily, sitting beside him on the bed. 'I'd just never seen a picture of your daddy before.'

Bobby yawned. 'He died when I was two. I only remember him when I look at the picture.' His eyes brightened again. 'Will you read me a story, Cori?'

'Oh, Bobby, I'd love to, but I have to see to Uncle Greg's supper. I'd be glad to any other night.'

'It's okay,' he said with a resignation unnatural for his age. 'Uncle Greg used to read to me, but he never has time any more now.'

Cori's hand came up to caress the dark hair from his forehead. 'My coming here changed a lot of things for you, didn't it, Bobby?'

His eyes opened wide. 'Oh, no, Cori. I'm glad you came and Uncle Greg married you ... you're nice ... and pretty ...'

'And it's time you went to sleep, young man!' Greg said from the doorway.

'Yes, Uncle Greg,' said Bobby, and surprisingly did so without further protest.

'He wanted me to read to him,' Cori said as they went down the staircase with its wrought iron railing, looking back into Greg's relaxed expression. 'Would you mind if I do that in future?'

'Not a bit. You'd probably make a better job of it than I ever did.'

'I doubt that, but I think Bobby needs some kind of personal care.' Then, wanting to clear him of any implied lack of care on his part, she added: 'I mean, his mother's away so much, and good as Ellen is it's not quite the same thing. She's so busy with other things.'

'That's true,' he agreed readily, looking intently into her eyes when they reached the hall. 'I'd be—grateful—for any mothering you can give him.'

A frown settled between Cori's brows as she went to the kitchen to deal with the steaks and salad. It was his own mother Bobby needed, not an uncle grateful for his pseudo-wife's pseudo-mothering. She forgot Bobby temporarily, however, when she carried the meal into the dining room and saw Greg's surprised look when she placed a sizzling, perfectly cooked steak before him.

'I didn't know you could cook,' he said in a puzzled voice.

Cori sat down opposite and spread her napkin on her knee. 'There's a lot you don't know about me,' she said lightly. 'I didn't always live in Howard Page's house, you know.'

'No, I suppose not,' he returned slowly. 'Where did you live?'

'I'll tell you while you eat,' she said, and proceeded to do so while he helped himself to crisp green salad. 'My father was an accountant ... reasonably successful, but never ambitious for money or power. He did some accountancy work for Howard's bank—that's how Doreen met him, she's good with figures and used to help Dad—and not long after they married, Dad got ill and needed a lot of nursing. So my mother did that while I took care of running the house and cooking the meals.'

'Weren't you at university?'

She shrugged. 'I dropped out for a year, and went back when Howard insisted on helping Mother and Dad to

retire to Arizona where the climate's better for his health
... Howard also paid for the rest of my education as well as
giving me luxurious room and board. In return, I helped
entertain Howard's important cl'ents'—a fleeting smile
touched her lips and eyes—'including you. Doreen always
hoped a well-heeled investor at the bank would come along
and fall for me.'

Greg said nothing for a moment, then lifted his glass of
full-bodied red wine and regarded her intently over it.
'And where did Roger fit into all this?' he asked quietly.

'Roger?' Cori's eyes dropped to her plate. 'He didn't.
Doreen was the happiest woman in the world when the ...
engagement was broken off. She wanted someone "better"
for me,' she ended on a bitter note.

'But you wanted to prove that somebody less well off—
like your father—was fine for you?'

Her lashes swept up over eyes widened in wonder. 'Maybe,' she said, slowly thoughtful. 'I don't know.'

'Mm. Well, let's eat. This steak is too good to spoil.'

They had almost finished their meal when the radio
telephone in the hall sounded with their signal. As their
eyes met in mutual question, Cori said:

'I'll get coffee while you answer that.'

It was impossible for her not to hear Greg's side of the
conversation as she carried the already perked coffee into
the dining room, and she abandoned her attempt to block
out his voice when she heard:

'I'll have to check with Cori ... hold on a second, Bill.'

His voice seemed unusually constrained when he came to
the dining room door and said: 'Some friends of mine,
Bill and Judith Anderson, are celebrating their sixth wedding anniversary next weekend, and they've asked us to go
down there. Would you like to?'

'Where is "down there"?' Cori asked, bewildered yet
aware that Greg wanted to go.

'They have a place not far from Williams Lake. We
could combine it with a shopping trip if there's anything
you need,'

'Yes, I'd like that,' she agreed readily. 'I'd like to meet your friends, too.'

He hesitated before going back to the phone. 'It—would mean a weekend down there.'

'Can Bobby come too?'

'Sure. They have a five-year-old boy—they expect Bobby to come.'

'Then that's fine. Ellen can have another weekend with her father.'

'Bill?' she heard him say as she poured coffee into cups. 'Yes, Cori would like to meet you two. She's been teaching school here, but that ends next weekend, so . . .'

The rest of his conversation was lost as the import of that statement hit her. Impossible to believe that she had been at the ranch for five weeks, and that next week would mark her last as a teacher there. She had grown fond of the Mason's Ridge children, from the pink and white plumpness of six-year-old Debbie to Jason with his shy, serious smile. Although she would still be here when school started again, Greg had found a teacher whose husband could work on the ranch. They would live in the sweet little house by the school, and perhaps sit out on the porch there in the evenings until the weather cooled. By the time snow drifted down across the valley, she herself would be back in Vancouver—looking back on her months at the ranch as a half-forgotten dream?

'I think you'll like the Andersons,' Greg interrupted her thoughts as he came back into the room, evidently satisfied with the conversation he had had with Bill.

'Have you known them long?'

'I went to school with Bill, then university . . . I was best man at their wedding . . . I'm godfather to their oldest son,' he told her in short statements.

'They sound like a very happy couple,' Cori remarked, putting cream in her coffee.

'They are. Very happy.'

A glow of triumph prompted her: 'So there *is* such a thing as romantic love?'

His eyes looked coolly into hers across the table, then he shrugged. 'They could be the exception that proves the rule.'

That the Andersons more than proved the rule was obvious to Cori from the start of the following weekend. Greg flew them into Williams Lake, where they transferred to the car he had ordered beforehand, and Cori spent a happy hour shopping in the central Cariboo town, buying several items she had run out of as well as a set of exquisitely cut crystal glasses as an anniversary gift.

The Anderson home, nestled at the edge of a small lake, was log built in the old style, resembling a Swedish chalet more than anything, but exuding the comforting warmth of a home where love abounded. Cori was surprised to see, because Greg hadn't mentioned it, that Judith was very obviously pregnant with their third child.

'Isn't it ridiculous to have a party at this stage of affairs?' she laughed to Cori as they entered the sprawling living room where stairs led to the upper storey. 'But Bill says he'll divorce me if I don't give him a daughter this time, so I thought I'd have one last fling.'

'I thought ranchers wanted sons,' Cori smiled, liking the older girl with her mid-brown hair cut short and merry brown eyes sparkling in her animated face.

'Well, that's so. but Bill says two boys are enough for a place this size. Now you, Greg,' the vivacious matron turned to Greg, 'you'll need at least six sons to cope with that place of yours—so watch out, Cori!'

Greg seemed to sense that Cori's throat had closed in embarrassment. 'Oh, I think four should do the trick,' he said smoothly, sliding an arm round Cori's waist and pulling her to his side. 'I don't want too much competition for my wife's attention.'

'Very wise,' Bill chuckled, his light-skinned face creasing in a rueful smile. 'Even with two, it's all I can do to get the time of day from Judith.'

Greg's brows lifted significantly in Judith's direction. 'That's a little hard to believe on the evidence.'

'This conversation's getting a little too personal for my liking,' Judith said with mock severity, turning to Cori. 'Come along upstairs, honey, and I'll show you your room. Greg knows it of old, so there's no need for him to come.'

A vague sense of disquiet began to possess Cori as she followed their hostess up the stairs to the upper floor. 'I'll show you your room', she had said ... stupidly, Cori had assumed that the room would be hers alone, but even before Judith opened the door on a small neat bedroom to the left of the hall, she knew she would be expected to share it with Greg as his wife. The barely double-sized bed. scarcely bigger than the one Greg occupied alone at Mason's Ridge, merely confirmed her worst fears.

'It's not very big,' Judith apologised, 'but my parents have the other guest room with twin beds. Anyway, I don't suppose a newly married couple like you and Greg will mind the togetherness.'

'No.' Cori forced a smile, wishing with all her heart that Judith's parents, obviously used to a normal married state, had opted for the more intimate bedroom. 'Wh-where will Bobby be?'

'Just next door in Tim's room.' Judith's head cocked to one side and she smiled. 'It's nice you care about Bobby ... his mother doesn't seem to very much.'

'Oh, I'm sure she does,' Cori defended quickly. 'It's just that ... with the talent she has ... she had to travel a lot.'

'Mm ... I've often thought it's a shame for Bobby that her talent doesn't run in more than that one direction.' Judith went with her awkward gait to the door. 'Tell me, does Marisa know about your marriage to Greg?'

'I don't—think so. Greg said she's travelling all over Europe, mostly just a night or so in each place.' An inexplicable pain had shot through Cori at mention of Marisa. If anyone knew about Greg's involvement with the pianist, she guessed it would be Greg's closest friends, and she forced a casual note to her voice when she added: 'Why? Do you think she'll object?'

Judith shrugged and made a sour face. 'Knowing Marisa,

she'll object very strongly to being pushed out of the lime-
light where Greg's concerned. But don't worry about her,
my dear—Greg's sensible enough to know that he has the
right wife for him. Can you really imagine Marisa Mason
as a ranch wife?' Her chuckle was cut off as sounds of
arrival came from outside the small square window. 'I'd
better go. If there's anything you need, Cori, let me know.
And come down as soon as you're ready—everybody's dying
to meet Greg's wife. We all thought he'd never marry. Not
that lots of girls haven't tried in the past, but he's never
been too interested.'

With a last smile, Judith went out, leaving Cori contemplating the small bed with increasing anger. Greg must
have known—or suspected—that this would happen. He
could have given her a warning, a choice of whether she
would come under these circumstances. Then she recalled
his hesitation when he had told her it would be a weekend
thing. How stupid she had been not to grasp the reason
for that hesitation!

Sighing, she wandered over to the window which looked
out to the front of the house where the lake glittered beyond the lawn. The ranch buildings to the right were fewer
than at Mason's Ridge, but all were meticulously neat with
white-painted rail fences contrasting with the dark red of
barns and stables.

Two men emerged from the biggest barn and came towards the house, one tall and dark and hatless, the other
shorter and stockier, his fair hair hidden under the wide-
brimmed hat that seemed uniform in these parts. It seemed
suddenly strange to observe Greg in these different surroundings, to see the flash of white teeth cutting across the
deep tan of his face as he greeted the new arrivals on the
lawn close to the lake's edge. Evidently he knew them well,
for he kissed the cheeks of the two women and chatted
easily with their husbands.

What would those women think if they knew he had
never kissed her, Cori, with sincerity like that? The two
he had given her at their wedding and the savage assault

on her lips the day after she came to Mason's Ridge could be discounted.

She saw his ask Judith something and his eyes immediately sought the window where Cori stood. She turned away quickly, but not before she saw him leave the group and come with long strides towards the house. In another minute he was framed in the small room's doorway.

'Why are you hiding away up here? Everybody wants to meet you.'

'To meet *me*, Greg? Or your wife?'

His brows drew down to almost meet in a black line across his eyes and he came fully into the room, closing the door behind him.

'Isn't it the same thing?' he asked quietly.

'You know it isn't,' she flared, suddenly angry as she paced back to the window and gestured to the people below. 'And they would know it too if I went down there and asked Judith for separate rooms because ... because ...' She floundered helplessly to a stop, her eyes dropping from his.

'Because we don't sleep together?' His voice was expressionless. 'If it's the one bed that's bothering you, don't worry. I intended to sleep on the floor.'

Her eyes went automatically to the dark-stained wood relieved only by a scatter rug here and there. 'You can't sleep on the bare floor!'

'I've slept on worse,' he said grimly. 'Now that's settled, will you come down with me?'

She stared at him for a moment longer, then nodded. 'I just have to write the card to go with the gift—or maybe you'd like to do it as they're your friends?' She stressed the 'your' and his mouth tightened.

'I think it would be better if you did,' he said evenly. 'Whatever our ... sleeping arrangements ... you're still my wife.'

While she bent over the maple dressing table to write a brief message on the card, he went downstairs to retrieve their luggage from the porch where he had left it on their arrival. Cori quickly ran a comb through her hair and touched up her lipstick, one that matched the coral of her pants suit, before Greg came back with her overnight case and his holdall, as well as the gift package for the Andersons. He seemed to take particular care to put their luggage at opposite sides of the room, and she breathed a little easier. Evidently he had no more desire for togetherness than she did.

Judith came into the lower hall as they emerged from the living room and smiled delightedly when Cori handed her the gift.

'We've all given up telling each other not to bring gifts because we always do anyway—and I refuse to be a hypocrite! I love getting presents.'

'So do I,' Cori smiled conspiratorially, glancing up hastily at Greg and surprising a thoughtful look in his eye.

'I think this bride of yours and I are going to get along really well, Greg,' said Judith, putting a hand on his arm. 'Thank you both so much, but I won't open it till Bill's here too. Why don't you two go on outside now? I just have a couple of things to do in the kitchen.'

Refusing Cori's offer of help, she shooed them out to where half a dozen couples chatted and laughed on the lawn, tall and cool-looking drinks in their hands. The talk died down when Cori appeared with Greg from the house, and eyes were frankly appraising as they approached. As if to seek reassurance, Cori put her hand under Greg's arm and felt the immediate comforting pressure as he squeezed it against his side.

Her fears were unfounded, however, and she was soon relaxed and enjoying the friendly acceptance around her, although she felt an occasional stab of guilt when she remembered how she was deceiving these friends of Greg's. They accepted her because she was the wife of a man they liked and respected ... somehow, she felt they would condemn her more than Greg for consenting to the deception.

'No wonder you've kept her locked away at the Ridge,

Greg,' one heavy-set man said with exaggerated awe. 'She's a real beauty.'

'That's not why he married her,' joked Bill, coming to hand Cori the drink she had asked for. 'I found out a little while ago that he had an ulterior motive ... isn't that right, Cori?'

For a moment her panicked eyes met Greg's and saw the barely perceptible shake of his head. Relieved, she turned back to Bill.

'You seem to know more than I do,' she said lightly. 'Why don't you tell me what his motive was?'

'Well, he needed a teacher as much as he needed a wife, so he killed two birds with one stone, didn't he?'

Cori wrinkled her nose at him. 'That's not very flattering, is it?'

The heavy-set man made a comforting noise. 'Don't you worry about that, honey. I'd stake anything I've got that Greg wouldn't have cared if you couldn't add up two and two. Teachers he can hire by the dozen—wives like you are a lot harder to come by.'

Cori was glad when Greg took her arm and led her to a newly arrived group, though the compliments there were just as fulsome. Strangely, the wives seemed not to resent their husbands' extravagant praise for Greg's new wife, all of them apparently pleased that the last remaining bachelor in their circle was settled in what they thought was a perfect marriage.

By the time the food was served on long tables under the trees, Cori felt she had known most of the guests for years. Only an occasional pinprick reminded her that in a month or two she would no longer be part of the friendly oneness of this ranching community. Even Bobby's occasional forays into the adult group with the oldest Anderson boy, Tim, had her as the obvious focus, cementing her even deeper into the unreal world of her marriage to Greg.

When at last the party broke up just before eleven, Cori found herself responding with enthusiasm to the many suggestions of a house party at Mason's Ridge.

'Couldn't we, Greg?' she asked, her eyes shining as she looked up to his face.

'If you'd like to, we'll arrange it,' he smiled back with unusual indulgence, his arm sliding round her waist. Although she knew it was a gesture meant to convince the others of their closeness, Cori relaxed against his side, feeling the vibrant heat of his body through the silk of her sleeveless top. 'But we'll have to do it in relays—we don't have enough beds for everyone here tonight, and it's too long a trip for a few hours' visit.'

An immediate chorus of: 'We'll bring our own sleeping equipment' vetoed the idea of separate visits, and Greg laughingly agreed to arrange the house party soon.

'Just think of all those lovely wedding gifts you'll get,' Judith drooled to Cori, adding belligerently: 'But don't you dare have your party before the baby arrives! That's one I want to be in on.'

When the last car had swept down the long driveway to the road, Judith's elderly parents said goodnight and went upstairs to bed, but the other two couples lingered on the porch companionably talking over the party. Judith relaxed on a rustic love-seat, Bill's arm round her, and Greg pulled Cori down beside him on a swinging couch opposite, one hand loosely holding hers on his knee. Just for show, Cori told herself, but she didn't mind at all the feel of his dry, warm skin resting lightly on hers, the hardness of his long thigh pressing against her soft flesh.

'Oh, go on, you two!' Judith interrupted herself to say in a half disgusted tone. 'You're sitting there almost like strangers, and you've hardly touched each other all day.' She looked adoringly up into Bill's face. 'When Bill and I had been married only six weeks, we were like Siamese twins, weren't we, darling?'

'Mm,' he grunted, adding sarcastically: 'But since then there seems to have been an obstacle or two coming between us.'

Judith laughed softly and subsided on his shoulder, her eyes going to the lake before them, glittering now with moonlight, so that she missed Greg's arm sliding round Cori's shoulders to pull her back against his chest. For a moment she stiffened, and he bent his head to whisper in her ear, his breath warm against her hair:

'Don't panic. It's just for a little while longer.'

Moonlight reflected as a deep gleam in his eyes when she raised her head to look at him, and something she saw there reassured her so that her body relaxed against him, her head leaning into the hollow of his shoulder. Across his chest she could see the lake and the half-fallen tree whose pendulous branches dipped into the water at its edge. Only the occasional eerie hoot of an owl disturbed the silence, a silence all four humans seemed unwilling to break.

Greg set the swing into gentle motion with his foot and a sigh escaped softly from Cori's lips. What a pity there wasn't a lake like this close to the house at Mason's Ridge.

'I could make one for you,' Greg murmured, making her aware that she had spoken aloud. 'It's possible I could divert the river, or at least draw a supply from it.'

'Could you?' She raised her head to look curiously at his slightly averted profile, moulded like granite against the lake yet having a certain softness round his well-shaped mouth. Only a man like Greg Mason would talk of diverting the massive power of a fast-flowing river for his own purposes, she mused. His half-lowered lids did little to hide the thoughtful action going on in his brain as it wrestled with the possible problems of filling an as yet non-existent lake, and she sighed again. Even if the lake did materialise at Mason's Ridge, she would not be there to see it—a fact he seemed to have forgotten in his absorption.

A child's terrified cry came from the open window of a room above the porch, shattering the drowsy silence, and Judith sat up away from Bill.

'That must be Tim,' she sighed tiredly. 'He's been dreaming a lot lately.'

'No, I think it's Bobby,' Cori cut in, rising quickly. 'I'll check, Judith, you stay where you are.'

Suddenly wide awake, she raced up the stairs and into the bedroom occupied by Bobby and Tim, not realising Greg had followed her until she heard his voice gently soothing Tim, who had been disturbed by Bobby's piercing cries. As she held Bobby's shuddering body in her arms, murmuring mindless comforts, he sobbed out the story of his nightmare against her neck in muffled gasps, still clutching her convulsively even when Greg came across to speak to him.

It was a long time before he was sufficiently soothed to be laid back on the pillow, his face wet with tears. Cori felt in her pockets for a facial tissue, then found Greg's handkerchief in her hand. Using it to dab away the tears from his cheeks and the perspiration from his hot brow, she said soothingly to Bobby:

'It was just a dream, darling, it's all finished now. Go back to sleep, and when you wake up in a little while it will be morning ... a nice sunny morning, and we'll swim in the lake. Then we'll go home to Mason's Ridge ... Uncle Greg and I are just next door if you need us ...'

A few minutes later when they went quietly from the room, Bobby fast asleep again, she handed the handkerchief back to Greg, and was surprised when his hand closed over hers to draw her out to the hall.

'Cori, I ...' He paused as if seeking for words, then seemed to abandon the search, substituting instead: 'Thanks for taking care of Bobby ... I couldn't have done it half as well.'

'Women are usually better at binding up knees and chasing away bogeymen,' she returned lightly, pulling her hand away and leaving the square of white linen in his. At that moment she didn't want to speculate on what he might have been going to say.

Bobby's nightmare broke up the remnants of the party, and when Cori at last mounted the stairs to the bedroom the full import of sharing that room with Greg descended on her like a suffocating pall. The trouble was, she told herself as she took her pale lemon short nylon nightdress from the case, that she had become too aware of Greg Mason as a man that day. Whatever Judith thought, their points of physical contact had been far more than normal, stimulating Cori's shallowly buried responses to an attractive man ... a very attractive man, she amended, fleeing to the bathroom and the sanctuary it offered while she showered.

Greg was in the bedroom when she eventually came back clutching to her throat the frothy negligée that matched her nightdress and wishing she had brought more conservative night attire. Another thought had struck her under the shower. She had discovered while making Greg's bed over the past weeks that he apparently wore no pyjamas while he slept, so she was relieved to see now that he had come equipped with at least pyjama trousers, which he had thrown casually over the bed.

He got up from the chair where he had been reading a thick paperback book, seeming annoyed about something as he indicated the bed and said: 'Will one blanket be enough for you if I take the other?'

'Y-yes, but ...' Cori took a deep breath and plunged on. 'I don't think you should sleep on the floor, Greg. For one thing it's too uncomfortable ... and for another I've told Bobby to come in if he needs us. If he does, Judith or Bill might come along too, and they'd think it ... odd if we ...'

He stared at her strangely for a long while before giving a curt nod. 'All right. I've no objection if you haven't.'

His indifference sparked a contrary sense of pique in Cori and she turned to look at herself in the dressing table mirror when he had taken up his pyjama trousers from the bed and his toilet gear from the holdall and disappeared. Why was he so unmoved—even hostile—to the idea of sharing her bed? Was she really so unattractive to him? Nothing she saw in the mirror could confirm that possibility.

The cascade of light brown hair flowing over her shoulders to frame a face which might not have set worlds afire

yet had been attractive to many men, she knew. Hazel
eyes fringed with dark lashes seemed a little larger than
normal, perhaps, but her nose still had its fine inward
curve at the bridge and delicately chiselled nostrils, her
mouth generously full over small, regular teeth. In a dream-
like state, she removed the negligée and surveyed her
figure critically. Breasts that were small but well formed
were barely visible at the low neckline of her gown. Roger
had often said that she could do with a few more pounds
here and there, leaving no doubt in her mind as to just
where he would have situated those extra pounds. Roger . . .

The mirror reflected the image of her startled eyes as
she realised that Roger, who had been the cause of her
broken heart just a few short weeks ago, seemed a remote
figure indeed, a pale figment from her past. It no longer
pained her to think about that final scene when he had
made it only too clear that his primary interest in her had
been fostered by his hopes of what Howard could do for
him in his career. An interest Greg had suspected without
even knowing Roger apart from a casual meeting. Greg . . .

For some strange reason Cori didn't want to think of
Greg Mason and his unusual perspicacity, and she picked
up the small bottle of perfume she had brought with her,
dabbing it lightly behind her ears and between her breasts.
However unattractive Greg might find her, she had no intention of spending her first night in bed with a man in an
unscented state!

She had just settled into bed and picked up the book she
had brought with her when Greg came from the bathroom,
his bare torso reddened from a vigorous towelling after his
shower. Did he always shave at bedtime? Cori wondered,
noting the smooth darkness of his determined chin. Strange
that she had been married to him for six weeks, and she
didn't know an elemental fact like that.

'I looked in on Bobby.' he said, disturbingly masculine as
he came towards the bed, his hair and chest darkness damp
from the shower. 'He seems to be all right now.'

She wondered if this was his way of telling her that he

was free to sleep on the floor after all, but when he had put away his things he came confidently to join her in the far from roomy bed, his weight pulling her like a magnet away from her own side.

'I'm glad,' she said quietly, lifting her book again and turning slightly away from him. 'He'll have forgotten all about his nightmare by morning.'

'What are you reading?' he asked indifferently as he picked up his own book.

'Oh, just something I picked up in your office,' she said casually, turning the book so that only the open pages were visible, but he stretched a lazy hand across her and read the title. '*Range Management*,' he mused thoughtfully. 'Are you thinking of going into competition?'

'Of course not. I don't understand a word of it—I thought it was something else.'

'Like what? *True Romance*?' he mocked, turning back to his own book. 'You won't find anything like that on *my* shelves!'

'I'm well aware of that!' she snapped, and turned on her side, her back an effective barrier to further conversation.

Although she had been determined to stay awake at least until he had gone to sleep, her eyes began to fuse over the incomprehensible text of the book she had foolishly picked up in an effort to understand and be able to talk about the intricacies of Greg's work. What did it matter anyway? In a few weeks, Greg Mason and all he stood for would be far behind her ...

CHAPTER SEVEN

CORI woke in a panic, fighting off the dead weight pinning her to the mattress, but however many times she succeeded in raising it, the weight fell back more heavily than ever over her body. Her head, too, seemed to be pinioned beside her, making movement impossible.

As her eyes adjusted to the dawn light filtering in at the unfamiliar square window, remembrance rushed over her ... Judith and Bill ... the party with all its new faces ... Bobby's nightmare ...

A deep groan close to her ear made her jerk her head round on the pillow. Greg's cheek lay against the spread curtain of her hair, his long and sinewy arm lay possessively across her, and he was obviously deep in a troubled sleep. Black brows dipped down to a deeply furrowed frown as he enunciated clearly:

'Marisa! Please, Marisa ...'

Cautiously, Cori raised herself on one elbow, wincing as her hair slid under his inert head. Her heart contracted when he groaned again and muttered words unintelligible to her. Without volition, her hand came up to touch and lie along the taut line of his jaw, her fingertips coming to rest just below his ear. Her puzzled eyes went over the bronze skin and mobile mouth, glancing over the proudly carved nose and up to the relative whiteness of the bear mark on his brow. Slowly, the knowledge came to her that it wasn't pity she felt for a man deep in the throes of a disturbing dream, as Bobby had been a few hours earlier. It was love. A love whose dimensions she had never gauged before, deep and everlasting and beautiful in its all-encompassing rightness ... a love doomed before it had bloomed, because Greg Mason had unconsciously made it clear that Marisa Mason was the woman of his dreams, the woman he loved.

He moaned again and moved his head restlessly, and Cori said with low urgency: 'Greg? Greg! You're dreaming ... wake up ...'

His eyes opened suddenly and clearly, looking directly into hers with a puzzled air.

'You're dreaming, Greg,' she repeated, her fingers tightening unconsciously on the prominent boniness of his lower jaw.

'I must be,' he said in a voice husky with sleep, his eyes making a slow wondering progress over her concerned face

and silky fall of hair that barely covered the exposed rise
of her breasts in the pale lemon nightdress. His dark lashes
remained lowered there for so long that she thought he
must be asleep again, but at last they rose to reveal eyes
that sought hers in wordless question.

She might have read a million things in those dark
depths, or nothing but the simple awakening of masculine
desire for an available female. Whichever it was, she was
powerless to do anything about the hand that came up to
tangle in the silken skeins of her hair and pull her head
inexorably down towards his face.

Like the velvet softness of rose petals joining the harsher
outer leaf, their lips met and held. Contented sweetness
poured through Cori's veins in the knowledge that this
was where she would always want to be, in the arms of the
man who could move her as no other could. Gone was the
harshness of his first kiss, his lips wooing her instead with a
tenderness and expertise she had not known existed in
him. Still less was she prepared for the wordless surge of
longing that rose from the deepest recesses of her being
when, without moving his lips from hers, he rolled her on
to her back and covered her body with the insistent urgency
of his.

His mouth became an instrument of persuasion, cajolery,
arrogant demand and persistent suing for her capitulation
... but not only her submission. His lips made it abun-
dantly clear that he wanted her response, her participation
to match the insistent demands of his body which his mind
normally controlled on a short leash. Time slipped away
from Cori, her eager response mindless in its ardency as
her hands ran over the smoothly muscled flesh of his back
and felt the cool thickness of his hair between her fingers.

Incoherent murmurs came from his lips when they left
her mouth and touched her ear, her eyes, her throat, and
moved purposefully down to the hardened rise of her
breast.

'No!' she cried, her voice strangled with the emotions
that gripped her. 'No, Greg!'

She wasn't the woman he wanted here, giving back the love he offered with abandoned freeness. The woman he was making love to was the one in his dreams ... Marisa ... the one he had called to.

Tears of regret, longing, bitterness filled her eyes and trickled down her cheeks. Greg, lifting his head from her breast, saw them and his face contorted in a paroxysm of rage.

'Damn you, Cori! Damn you to hell!'

With one violent movement he threw back the covers and leapt from the bed, scooping up his clothes on his way to the door. Cori's breath came in gulping sobs when it had closed behind him. Never in her life had she felt so miserable, so desolate, as she did at that moment.

The flight back to Mason's Ridge after lunch was eventful and accomplished mostly in silence, even Bobby seeming to be digesting the weekend just past. When Greg had to speak, it was mostly in bitten-off monosyllables that indicated that his mood was no better than it had been during the morning.

Cori turned her head away in the seat beside him, but the breathtaking splendour of the scenery unfolding beneath them might have been desert. Greg's attitude puzzled her. Although she had spent most of the morning in the lake with the children, teaching the youngest Anderson boy the rudiments of swimming, her brief contacts with Greg convinced her that she had offended him deeply by crying when he was making love to her. But why?

It would perhaps have been easier to understand if theirs had been a usual marriage, contracted for normal reasons. But it hadn't been. Greg had made it clear that physical attraction was all that drew a man and woman together. Surely, then, he shouldn't feel so rejected because she hadn't chosen to go along with his thinking? Especially when that thinking had been invoked by his dreams of another woman?

She gave an unconscious sigh and turned back to the

wide front window, sensing Greg's quick glance in her direction but determinedly staring straight ahead.

'We're almost home now, aren't we, Uncle Greg?' Bobby piped up from the rear seat, his jubilant voice bearing no remembrance of his nightmare of the night before.

'Five minutes,' Greg said tersely.

'Look, Cori, there's the logging camp—see the little buildings?'

Cori's eyes swept over the gently sloping hill to their right, seeing the evidence of logging activity in the fallen trees half way up the slope, the cluster of buildings huddled closely together in the lower valley.

'It seems such a shame to cut down those lovely old trees,' she said unthinkingly, her head swivelling to meet Greg's hard look when he said coldly:

'We're very selective in clearing the slopes. No one area ever looks as if it's been scalped.'

No, it wouldn't, she thought ruefully. Not with Greg Mason directing operations. His love for this country was greater than he would ever own for a woman ... even Marisa.

Two minutes later Greg uttered a muffled oath as Bobby shouted: 'There's another plane coming in to land at the Ridge ... somebody's coming to visit!' He was silent for a few moments while Greg banked their plane and followed the commercially marked Cessna down to the landing strip. 'Will it be Mommy coming to see us?'

'I can't think who else it would be,' Greg muttered, negotiating a bumpier landing than Cori had experienced with him so far. But then Marisa Mason had never been waiting for their arrival before!

They came to a halt not far from the other plane, and Bobby could barely contain his excitement while Greg lifted him down from his seat. In another moment he was running across the gravel strip towards the woman who had just descended from the Cessna, calling: 'Mommy! Mommy!'

Even without Bobby's confirming shouts Cori would have

recognised the svelte darkness of Marisa Mason, a darkness made more absolute by the white suit she wore. Cori felt a moment of panic, a deep reluctance to go forward towards the woman who meant so much to Greg. But his hand was at her elbow, grasping it with a bruising hold that said much more than the words he spoke.

'Remember, you're my *wife*!'

As his arm urged her forward, Cori's scattered thoughts marshalled themselves together. The reason for her being here—for being Greg Mason's wife—was to face this woman who threatened to disrupt the life of the little boy Cori had come to love. When it had happened, or how, she didn't know, but suddenly she was aware that the boy's welfare was uppermost in her mind as it was in Greg's.

Nut brown eyes went dismissingly over her as they approached the obvious target of those animated orbs being Greg's tightly held figure and strongly hewed face. Cori had a fragmented impression of smooth, Madonna-like features reaching up like an early sun to the sky, of finely chiselled lips touching and holding to Greg's far longer than would a normal sister-in-law's.

A small muscle played along the line of Greg's jaw as he put his hands on Marisa's arms and thrust her from him, his eyes shrouded with unfathomable emotion. Putting one arm round Cori's waist to draw her forward, he said:

'Marisa, I'd like you to meet Cori ...' he paused, his eyes narrowing to hard watchfulness, '...my wife.'

The brown-eyed gaze was directed straight into the darker blackness of his, not a muscle of the perfectly composed features betraying a sign of surprise.

'Your—*what*?'

'My wife,' Greg repeated stiffly, but Cori seemed to detect a faint note of triumph as he added, turning his head to look down into her face: 'Cori, this is my sister-in-law, Marisa ... Bobby's mother.'

'How—how do you do?' Cori stammered, uncertain whether to put out her hand in greeting, but the other woman's continued and calculating scrutiny of Greg's features froze her arms to her sides.

'Your wife,' Marisa said in a flat voice that hinted of steel although it was velvet soft. She gave a laugh that was half admiring. 'I see what your game is, Greg, but it won't work.'

'It's worked very well so far—hasn't it, honey?' he turned again to give Cori a slow smile of intimacy, his arm tightening round her waist to pull her closer against his side. She wondered if Marisa, too, could see the cold gleam deep in his eyes, but made a supreme effort to respond suitably to his act of loving husband. This meeting with Marisa was the severest trial so far of their ability to carry off the impression of a normal marriage. Her arm came up round Greg's waist at the back, and she leaned her head against his shoulder to smile with her lips and eyes up into his face.

'Very well, darling,' she murmured huskily, and reached up to touch his cheek fleetingly with her lips. The only problem was, she thought disconsolately, feeling the harshness of his beginning growth of beard against her tender skin, the acting was only on his side. There was no artifice in her need to lean against the tall hardness of his lean frame. But as if he sensed this, he put her away from him when Bobby said from beside his mother:

'Here's Hank with the jeep ... can I sit with you, Mommy?'

'You can sit in the back with what's her name,' Marisa snapped irritably, ignoring his crestfallen face as Hank drew to a dust-provoking halt close by.

Cori smiled stiffly at Hank as he leapt from the driving seat and came across to the small group. While he greeted Marisa with tempered enthusiasm, Cori went to take her place at the rear of the jeep, but felt herself being lifted bodily into the front seat.

'I say who goes where around here,' Greg said in a gritty voice. 'Your place is beside me.'

Giving her no time to reply, he wheeled round and crossed with rapid strides to where the pilot of the chartered plane leaned nonchalantly against the fuselage. After a few minutes of conversation, the pilot climbed back into the cockpit and taxied off down the strip.

Meanwhile, a frozen-faced Marisa had installed herself beside Bobby in the rear seat of the jeep, making known her disapproval of being relegated a back seat by maintaining an icy silence, even in the face of Bobby's excited chatter about all he wanted to show his mother.

But at last even Bobby sensed the strained atmosphere between the adults, and when Greg came back to take his seat behind the wheel he put the jeep savagely into gear and accomplished the short journey to the ranch in grim silence. Cori felt Marisa's dark gaze boring through the thickness of her brown fall of hair, but reflected that perhaps her imagination was working overtime because of the bad start to their relationship. A relationship that promised to remain static, Cori told herself wryly, if beginning conditions were any indication.

At the house, Greg started up the stairs with part of Marisa's luggage and Cori murmured to him: 'I'll see to the room.'

'Where's Ellen?' Marisa demanded loudly from the hall.

'She went to see her father, who hasn't been well, in their village,' Cori explained. 'We've been away for the weekend, so there wasn't any reason——'

'Oh, God,' Marisa raised her eyes heavenward. 'Her cooking's nothing to rave about at the best of times, but at least it's filling. I'm starved!'

'I think I can rustle something up,' Cori consoled, thankful for her own foresight in leaving a sizeable beef roast in the refrigerator to defrost while they were away.

'Oh, you cook too, do you?' Marisa said insultingly, about to add something else when Cori turned her back and went up the stairs.

Greg stood in the middle of the large two-windowed room above the living room, obviously unaware of Cori's footsteps on the thick pile carpet. His eyes were directed to the huge bed situated between the two windows, the side of his jaw that she could see working convulsively. Pain shot through her, leaving her breathless. That Marisa's presence affected him deeply was patently obvious—how deeply and how obviously was evident in the naked emotion his eyes reflected when he spun round as she spoke.

'I'll see to the room if you'd like to go down and entertain your sister-in-law,' she said in as crisp a voice as she could muster. 'Will she expect to have her things unpacked for her?'

'She can do it herself!' he said, surprising her with the savagery of his tone. 'Cori?' he called after her retreating figure as she went to get fresh sheets from the linen closet.

'Yes?'

When she turned to face him, forcing coolness to her manner, he seemed at a loss for words. One long bronzed hand raked through his black hair and his brow knitted in a perplexed frown when he came to stand close to her.

'Cori, I—I know it isn't going to be easy for you, having Marisa in the house. There are—things I haven't told you. Things that maybe you should know.'

'It's all right, Greg,' she said in a voice that betrayed none of the heartache she was feeling. 'Our agreement didn't mean we have to bare our souls to each other—remember?'

He flinched as if she had struck him, then his mouth compressed into a tight line. 'Yes, that's so.' Flatly, he asked: 'Can you manage dinner as well as everything else?'

She shrugged. 'I've coped with more. But I'll have to get started now, if you'll excuse me.'

When she came back from the linen closet with the daintily flowered polyester sheets, Greg had gone and, repressing the imagination that tended to conjure up emotion-fraught scenes taking place below, she made up the bed and checked that everything was in place.

The rest of the afternoon and early evening passed in a haze of preparation for the meal Cori had determined would be a success in a culinary sense if no other. Marisa staved off hunger with the ham sandwiches Cori made for her, and she and Greg spent most of the time conversing in low voices in the living room.

Bobby seemed subdued when she called him to the kitchen for his evening meal of hamburger patties, mashed potatoes and carrots fresh from Joseph's garden plot.

'Mommy doesn't want to see my hamsters and fish 'quarium,' he told her dolefully, pushing the food dispiritedly round his plate.

'Of course she does,' Cori smoothed, casting a supervisory look at the roast in the oven before coming to sit opposite him at the dinette table. 'She's just tired after travelling all day. Tomorrow she'll want to see everything.'

Bobby gave her an old-fashioned look from the corner of his eyes. 'If you had a little boy and you hadn't seen him for a long, long time, would you be too tired to see his hamsters and fish?'

Cori's heart lurched uncomfortably. If she had a little boy ... Greg's son would look quite like Bobby, with those dark eyes and hair and appealing childishly rounded cheeks that showed promise of the good-looking man to come. On a more practical level, she said:

'I'm sure my little boy would understand why I wanted to wait till I was rested before seeing all his things.' Taking the fork from his hand, she scooped a portion of food from his plate to hold before his lips.

'Would he?' Greg's voice came quietly from the door before his gracefully lazy figure crossed to sit beside Bobby. His eyes lingered for a moment on Cori's, then he took the fork from her hand and looked away only to place the contents between Bobby's suddenly parted lips. 'Yes, Bobby, I think Cori's son would know that his mother loved him enough to let him wait to show her all his precious things.'

Bobby chewed thoughtfully, his eyes on his uncle's, then swallowed. 'If Cori had a little boy he would be your little boy too, wouldn't he, Uncle Greg?'

For a fraction of a second black eyes met light hazel before Greg drawled: 'Yes, I guess that's so. Just like you're my boy, Bobby.'

Bobby shook his head definitely. 'No, you're not my daddy—but you'd be his daddy, wouldn't you?'

Greg carefully put another forkful to the boy's lips. 'Yes. But your daddy was my brother, so that's nearly the same thing, isn't it?'

'I guess so.' Bobby's face brightened. 'Then Cori would be like my mommy, wouldn't she?'

Greg stood suddenly, seeming tall beside the table. Cori, without daring to look up at him, said crisply: 'You have a mother, Bobby, so you don't need me for that. I—I'm just your aunt, and you should never forget that.'

'Yes, Cori,' Bobby said in a small voice, taking up the abandoned fork and plying it himself. By the time he had raised it to his mouth, both Cori and Greg had disappeared from the vicinity of the table.

The rich notes of the grand piano filled the living room while Cori curled up in her favourite corner of the sofa close to Greg's chair, sipping the liqueur he had poured for her.

A week had gone by since Marisa's arrival, and it had become a regular thing for the three adults to gather in the living room with their coffee after dinner, two to listen while the other played.

Every evening Cori sat enraptured by the professional performance given for her and Greg alone ... although something about the transformed features of Marisa's face indicated her own pleasure in becoming lost in the music that was her life. The sharp yet dulcet tones of the Chopin Nocturnes were followed by a repertoire encompassing Beethoven, Mozart, Debussy, in an unending stream of pure and seemingly effortless talent. Greg, too, seemed absorbed by the music, although his face was usually impassive as he nursed his brandy glass and listened while thse frail Madonna-like creature coaxed unbelievable cadences from the piano.

On this particular evening, however, Cori let the music flow over her to form a background for her disturbing thoughts. The half uneasy truce that had been established between herself and Marisa permitted no more than a restrained politeness between them when they were forced into each other's company. Cori had forsaken the soothing coolness of the glittering pool when Marisa, complete with all the paraphernalia she seemed to require to sit by the pool, installed herself in a lounge chair and paid little or no attention to Bobby's efforts to impress her with his accomplishments.

It was at night, under the dominant maleness of Greg's presence, that Marisa shone. Even Cori had to admit that Ellen's uninspired cooking took on a new aspect under Marisa's sparkling conversation. Greg appeared not to notice what he ate as the slightly husky voice recounted tales of happenings on her concert circuit.

Apart from a faintly mocking look in the liquid brown eyes whenever Greg touched or addressed Cori intimately, Marisa had made no direct comment to Cori about the hasty marriage contracted between her brother-in-law and a girl he had scarcely known. Until this evening ...

Marisa, unusually early for the pre-dinner drink, had already been installed in the living room when Cori entered it, and from the flashing look she threw at Cori the drink on the table beside her chair was not her first.

'So,' she mocked, 'the bride appears! A bride ... yet not a bride. How does it feel, my dear, to be the wife of a man who cares nothing for you? A man who's using you for his own ends.'

Cori walked to the bar and poured herself a drink, conscious of the now venomous eyes on her figure which was made even more slender by the cut of her dress that fell in soft peach folds to her feet.

'I don't know what you mean.' She forced herself to walk unhurriedly to the sofa and take her seat as far away as possible from Marisa's chair. How she wished that Greg would put in his appearance, but she knew that he would not for some time ... he had come home late after a long day away from the ranch. Not in the best of moods either, if the banging of doors when he entered the master wing was any indication.

'You know what I mean all right,' Marisa sneered. 'All these little loving touches don't fool me one bit!' Her gaze became speculative, her tone thoughtful. 'I can see Greg's reason for marrying you, but your motive escapes me. You come from a wealthy background, I understand, so it couldn't have been a case of grabbing the first well-to-do man who came along.'

'Is it so hard to believe that I might have fallen in love with Greg? He's a very attractive man.' Cori's hand tightened on her glass.

The dark eyes narrowed. 'Oh, yes, I can believe you're in love with him—now! But not when you married him.' Marisa rose suddenly and paced to the bar to replenish her drink. 'It won't do you any good though, sweetie. Greg isn't in love with you, and he never will be. You know why, don't you?'

A flutter of disquiet beat with tiny wings in Cori's stomach, but her outward composure remained. 'Suppose you tell me?'

'Because he loves me!' Marisa threw out fiercely, coming to bend slightly over Cori's seated figure. 'He's always wanted me, from the first time his brother brought me here. John knew that ... and that I wanted Greg, too.'

'It must have been convenient for you both when ... John died,' Cori said drily. 'Why didn't you get together then?'

Marisa turned away and went moodily back to her chair, sipping from her glass before answering. 'Conscience! When John was killed, Greg knew it was his fault. The bear went for him first and John drew its attention away from Greg to himself ...' Her eyes widened. 'Hasn't he told you how that scar on his head came about?'

Cori licked suddenly dry lips. 'Only ... that he'd been

... attacked by a bear. I didn't know his brother had been ... killed ... in the same accident.'

There was triumph in Marisa's smile 'That proves my point, doesn't it?—about his conscience. He'd have told you about it, surely, if he'd had nothing to hide.'

'Hide? Why should he have anything to hide? It could have been the other way round—he might have been killed saving John.'

Marisa's eyes took on a false glaze of surprise. 'But of course he wouldn't have told you that either. John wasn't killed by the bear ... he was shot to death!'

CHAPTER EIGHT

UNABLE to bear her thoughts any longer, Cori rose and went to the long doors leading off to the porch, passing through them to stand with one arm circling one of the white roof supports. Stars bigger than any she had seen in the city spread a brightly studded black canopy over the hills and plain ...

Greg owned it all, this husband who was becoming increasingly and frighteningly ... a mystery to her. He loved the ranch, of that she was sure. Enough to kill the older brother who would normally have inherited it? That he had a savage streak in his nature was beyond doubt—his first kiss, devoid of feeling, had shown her that. Or was his love for Marisa alone enough to kill for her? She jumped when Greg's quiet voice came from behind.

'Cori? Is anything wrong?'

'I—I—nothing,' she stammered. catching a glimpse of moonlight gleaming in his eyes as she turned back to the front. Yes, it would be only too easy to imagine that he would do anything to gain what he wanted. That he had refrained from marrying Marissa because of a belated conscience was a very slender point in his favour.

'There is something,' he insisted, feeling her shiver

when he put a hand on her elbow to turn her round to face him. 'What is it? Has Marisa been saying something to you?'

'N-no.' Frantically, Cori cast around in her mind for something to say. 'Just that she doesn't believe we're really ... man and wife.'

'Oh?'

She glanced up to his shadowed face, her eyes meeting and holding to his in an invisible lock, and hated herself for her body's response to his nearness. The pale plaid of his shirt threw into relief his dark features, the firm muscles of his fit body warmly taut against hers. His head lifted slightly as the piano notes ceased abruptly, and his mouth bent then to Cori's.

'Then maybe we should be a little more convincing,' he murmured against her lips, his arms gliding round the silky material of her dress as he pulled her harder against him. There was no time for protest, no time to think before his mouth covered hers, parting her lips and moving his own with deliberate sensuousness over them. One of his hands, each finger a hard shaft, tangled in her hair to hold her head steady ... but that was unnecessary.

Even the outraged gasp that came from the open doors a few yards away failed to stop the dizzy spiral Greg's kiss induced. Cori's eyes were closed, but still the hard brilliance of the stars revolved glitteringly in her darkened brain. Heat sprang like a forest fire from his body to hers as she arched eagerly against him and knew that his desire equalled, or even outmatched, her own.

'How touching!' Marisa's harshly taunting voice penetrated the aura surrounding them. 'Your act is almost convincing tonight.'

Greg's head lifted slowly from Cori's, and though his words were addressed to Marisa, his eyes remained fixed on Cori's with the same surprised question she had noticed on their wedding day. As if ...

'That was no act, Marisa. Surely you're experienced enough to know that?'

The dark woman laughed huskily as she sauntered over to them. 'I'm experienced enough in *your* ways to know that you'd do anything to keep Bobby here—can you deny that?'

Now he did look away from Cori's luminous eyes, releasing her suddenly so that she swayed back against the white post. 'No,' he admitted tersely, 'I won't deny I want Bobby at Mason's Ridge—and you know why.'

'Oh, yes,' she mocked softly. 'I know why. But does your little bride know why?'

His voice came out through stiff lips. 'Cori knows as much as she needs to.'

'But do you think that's fair, darling? Surely, as you're wife, she should know—*everything* about you!'

Suddenly sickened by the barbed exchange, which was going on as if she was non-existent, Cori drew herself up and brushed past Greg, making for the glass doors.

'Excuse me,' she muttered wildly, 'I have a headache.'

Ignoring the command in Greg's: 'Cori!' she went as if her feet had wings across the living room and along the passage to her room, pausing there to lean tremblingly against the ornately scrolled dressing table.

Her head really did ache as it whirled with all the confusing messages it had had to absorb that day. First, Marisa's more than broad hint that Greg had killed his brother because he desired her ... Cori's own mindless response to his kiss which was, in spite of his denial, an effort to prove to Marisa that their marriage was normal ... his obvious desire to keep from her the things Marisa had said Cori ought to know ...

'Hank, would you be willing to fly me into Williams Lake?' Cori asked innocently the next day. She had ostensibly gone down the hill to seek vegetables from Joseph, knowing that Greg had gone to check second cut grasses in valleys lying far to the north-west and that Hank had not gone with him.

Hank pushed his clay-coloured hat to the back of his

head and regarded her with the faint tinge of admiration he had shown since her arrival as Greg's wife, mingled with a countryman's caution of getting in over his head.

'Greg's going in tomorrow to get the mail and supplies,' he said warily. 'Couldn't it wait till then?'

'No, it couldn't.' His brows lifted at her sharp tone, and she went on hurriedly: 'You see, I—well, it's a surprise for his birthday. It wouldn't be a surprise, would it, if he takes me there? I know exactly what I want,' she warmed to her spur of the moment excuses, 'so we could be back before he knows we're gone. He said it would be late afternoon before he gets home. Will you take me, Hank?'

Whether it was because her eyes widened appealingly on his, or that he welcomed a few hours off from ranch chores, Hank agreed to take her.

'If you can be ready in half an hour, we can be back in good time before Greg. I'll pick you up at the house.'

'Thanks, Hank,' she smiled, the guilt she felt at using the affable foreman in her scheme for escape from Mason's Ridge evaporating as she walked up the hill to the house and recalled the conversation she had heard the night before.

Going from the master suite along the carpeted corridor leading to the living room, she hadn't realised she was eavesdropping until it was too late to turn back.

'... inexperienced girl doesn't mean anything to you,' Marisa's faintly husky voice was saying. 'Not after all we've been to each other.'

'What have we been to each other, Marisa?' Greg's half amused, half annoyed words floated out to Cori. 'Two people drawn together by a mutual interest ... Bobby!'

'You know there's a lot more than Bobby between us,' Marisa said passionately. 'Or there could be if you'd ... Greg, I've been thinking. I'm getting tired of travelling all over the place, playing a night here, two nights there. Now might be a good time for me to retire ... to be the wife of a dedicated rancher who doesn't care to travel the world with me. What do you say to that?'

'I already have a wife,' Greg returned tersely. Cori glimpsed his lean frame, dressed completely in black as on the first night she had spent at Mason's Ridge, at the bar as he poured himself another drink.

'Don't be ridiculous, darling,' Marisa said dismissingly. 'We all know why you married her. But that reason doesn't exist if ... you and I ...'

Cori's eyes felt bruised when she saw the darkly petite woman, dressed in a stark white dress that contrasted sharply with the black of Greg's clothes, melt against him. Blindly, she turned and went back to the room that had become a haven for her, a protection against the hurts lying in wait beyond the white-painted door.

Now as she reached the top of the rise and paused to look out across the valley she reflected sadly that no one at Mason's Ridge would miss her ... except Bobby, perhaps, but it would be better for him to be free of his dependency on Cori and turn to his mother for his needs. He would have had to do that in any case after the custody hearing was over.

Sighing, she went into the house. She couldn't even say goodbye to Bobby because he was spending the day with friends on the lower level. There was no sign of Marisa in the downstairs rooms, only the sound of Ellen's tuneless voice humming as she went about her duties in the kitchen. Swallowing the lump in her throat, Cori decided it was best to say nothing to Ellen either.

Hank seemed exhilarated when he came to pick Cori up, and she gathered as they drove across to the airstrip that this was brought about by the prospect of his paying an unexpected visit to a girl he knew in Williams Lake.

Cori hadn't dared to pack any of her clothes, knowing that Hank's suspicions would have been immediately aroused, but that was the least of her worries. Right now, all she wanted to do was to put space—lots of space—between herself and Mason's Ridge. Not even Greg would come after the wife who had left him; his proud nature would never let him humble himself before the conventionally straight Howard and Doreen.

As she waited for Hank to taxi the plane from the silver-hued shed at the end of the strip Cori thought she saw a puff of dust from the flat far down the valley, but then her attention was engaged in installing herself beside Hank in the four-seater plane. Just as he was about to set the plane into motion, however, the passenger door was thrown violently open.

'Just where do you think you're going?' Greg ground out with ominously lowered voice, his strong hands coming up to remove Cori bodily from the plane.

'Hell, Greg, it's supposed to be a surprise for your birthday!' Hank protested, his face red as he killed the engine.

'It's supposed to be a surprise all right,' Greg returned grimly. 'Put the plane away and ride my horse back to the ranch. I'll talk to you later.'

'It's not Hank's fault,' Cori said indignantly as Greg bundled her into the jeep with firm hands. 'I asked him to take me so that I could buy your—birthday present.'

'You're a little premature,' he said drily, getting into the driving seat beside her. 'My birthday isn't until February next year.'

'How was I supposed to know that?' she cried wildly. 'You never tell me anything!'

He said no more then, but tightened his jaw and drove like a maniac over the rutted bumps until he drew the jeep to a halt under the shade of trees sparsely distanced some way from the ranch. His voice, though held in check, seemed loud in the sudden silence when he cut off the engine.

'You were running away,' he stated flatly without looking at her, his arms a dark bronze in short-sleeved shirt as he grasped the wheel. 'You were running out on our agreement. Why?'

Then he looked at her, and Cori was shocked by the ravaged look deep in his eyes. Her knuckles grew white as her fingers dug into the seat under her.

'I—there's no reason for our agreement now,' she whispered at last.

'Why should you think that?'

'Well, I—I overheard Marisa telling you last night that . . . .'

His head nodded in sudden clarification. 'So that's why I had to come and root you out of your room for dinner?' Bleak anger replaced the rawness in his eyes. 'How much of that conversation did you hear?'

Until you took her into your arms and forged a new agreement with Marisa, she wanted to cry, but instead said in a low voice: 'Enough to know that—Marisa's willing to give up her career to marry you. That makes our agreement null and void, doesn't it?'

A muscle played along the smooth line of his jaw and he looked away from her. 'That sounds like a legal term you might have picked up from your ex-fiancé!' he sneered. 'What were you planning to do?—take up with him where you hadn't left off?'

'Maybe,' she threw back recklessly, knowing that he was ignorant of the contents of Doreen's letter of a week ago telling her that Roger was now engaged to her replacement. The news had shocked Cori only because her reaction to it had pointed up how remote and unreal Roger had become in her mind. In a matter of weeks her emotions, her perceptions, had been flooded with a man—and a country —that were larger than life itself. 'But that's my business . . . it can't possibly concern you.'

'That's just where you're wrong,' he snapped, turning hardened eyes to the nettled flash in hers. 'It happens to be very much my business . . . for the present. You've made an agreement with me, and I intend to see that you stick to it. Once this thing with Bobby is settled, you can go wherever you damn well please. Until then you stay here, even if I have to lock you up!'

'That's hardly necessary, is it?' Cori questioned bitterly. 'Hank isn't likely to be persuaded to take me out of here now! Doesn't it worry you,' she went on curiously, glancing up at the stern lines of his face, 'what interpretation Hank's putting on that scene just now?'

'He's paid to interpret my orders regarding the ranch, not my marital affairs.'

It was hard to believe at that moment that those tightly compressed lips had kissed her with a warmth that barely concealed the savage underlying passion she sensed he was capable of. But then he had admitted that no scales of false romanticism clouded his gaze when he desired an attractive woman ... and Cori knew that she had a certain attractiveness for him. Nothing to approach the emotional hold Marisa had on him, but ...

Hopelessly, her anger gone, she said: 'Why don't you marry Marisa and be done with it, Greg? It would solve all your difficulties ...'

'*If* and *when* I take a real wife,' he began harshly, his eyes raking over her slender figure contemptuously, 'I'll do the proposing. Marisa and I have ties that go back a long way, but ...'

'All the way back to your brother's death?' she threw in without thinking, and shrank back against the seat when he swivelled round sharply to glare at her savagely.

'Who's been talking about that?' he demanded, the glitter in his eyes maniacal enough to make Cori shiver and believe him capable of murdering for something he wanted badly. 'Marisa? What did she tell you?'

'J-just that you—your brother was—killed at the same time as you—as the bear attacked you.'

'That's all she told you?' His eyes bored into hers for another moment, and then he seemed satisfied with her wordless nod, turning back to the front again to stare sightlessly through the trees.

'I'm sorry, Greg ... I didn't know——'

'There's nothing for you to know,' he said tersely, starting the engine in one swift movement. 'What happened that day concerns only Marisa, and me, and ... Bobby.'

He drove back to the house in silence, scarcely waiting for Cori to get out of the jeep before roaring off to the working part of the ranch below. Cori stumbled across the forecourt to where she could see the vehicle go with dangerous speed down the steep incline as if a devil drove Greg Mason.

Was it the devil of conscience, as Marisa had told her? His unwillingness to discuss the circumstances of his brother's death could have one of two reasons. Either he had been so close to his brother that raking over the details of his death was painful to Greg—or guilt at having momentarily given way to the temptation to get rid of the only obstacle to his love for Marisa. A guilt that now made him fanatical in his protection of his fatherless nephew.

Cori went into the house and along to the master suite in a daze. Her heart wanted to believe that the first alternative was the right one, but logic reminded her that Greg, who had his emotions under tight control most of the time, would have accepted the tragic accident of his brother's death long before now ... if it had been an accident. The other alternative didn't bear thinking about ...

Another week passed, a week of day-long sunshine so hot that Cori eventually capitulated and swam in the inviting coolness of the pool. Marisa's dark-skinned body grew darker under the ministrations of sun and vast amounts of sun-tan lotion she lavished on it, but she had been strangely subdued since the night Cori had heard her offer herself to Greg as his wife. Her attitude to Cori, while no warmer, was more wary, as if she felt she had underestimated the younger girl's influence with Greg.

Greg himself seemed to foster this idea by being more attentive to Cori, even taking a seat beside her on the sofa in the evenings and ignoring her cool stiffness when his arm slid across her shoulder, his hand lying with casual warmth on her upper arm. Much harder for her to ignore was the vibrant masculine firmness of his body as it pressed against her side, and several times she gave in to her fanciful wish that this was a genuine relationship by relaxing her neck muscles against the line of his arm behind her head.

Bobby, resigned now to his mother's indifference to his prowess in the pool, cavorted playfully with Cori in the water, even extracting fun from her efforts to teach him lifesaving techniques.

One day, having stubbed his toes painfully against the concrete sides of the pool, it was Cori he turned to for comfort and she was still cradling his head against her when Greg appeared suddenly in the open doorway. He looked hot in khaki denim and said irritably to Marisa, whose head was buried in a magazine: 'What's wrong with Bobby?'

'Bobby?' she said vaguely, pulling down her sunglasses to look across at her son, who had stemmed his tears at the sound of his uncle's voice. 'Why don't you ask your wife about that? She seems to have taken him over too.'

The 'too' hung in the air as Greg's eyes swivelled back to the slender girl seated at the side of the pool, one arm still round his nephew's fine-boned frame.

'Bobby hurt his toes,' Cori explained quietly, 'but you're fine now, aren't you, honey?'

As if to prove her statement, Bobby jumped to his feet and ran across to Greg, leaving wet footprints on the tile. 'Cori's been teaching me how to lifesave, Uncle Greg, but we need somebody to practise on—will you come in the pool with us?'

For a moment it seemed Greg would refuse, but a gleam came to his eyes when Cori's head turned away in embarrassment. 'All right,' he said, 'give me a minute to change.'

To Cori it seemed less than a minute before he reappeared, bronzed and muscular in brief swimming shorts, poising himself over the deep end momentarily before plunging cleanly into the water. Her eyes happened to glance over in Marisa's direction and she saw that the other woman had missed none of the masculine perfection of Greg's body as he knifed into the clear blue of the pool. Slightly sickened by the bared longing in Marisa's eyes, Cori drew her long legs from the water and stood on the tile preparatory to leaving the scene, but Greg's realistic splutters close by made her pause and look down into the churning water.

'Uncle Greg's drowning!' Bobby squealed with unseemly glee. 'We have to save him, Cori.'

Cori had no choice but to follow the olive brown limbs into the pool ... Greg was, after all, simply reinforcing her own earlier instruction ... and she marvelled at his acting ability as he at last lay supine on the tiles giving every impression of a drowning man. But then, she thought sourly, she had every reason to know that he was a superlative actor!

'Do we breathe into his mouth now, Cori?' Bobby asked, slightly awed by his uncle's realistic performance.

'No,' she said, an imp of mischief lighting the hazel of her eyes as she knelt beside the virile healthiness of Greg's tanned body. 'First we have to check for false teeth and take them out.'

Bobby giggled while Greg half opened one eye to glare balefully at her.

'Uncle Greg doesn't have false teeth,' Bobby chuckled. 'Look, they're all fixed.' His small fingers pried apart the well shaped lips and tugged at the strong white teeth behind them.

'Oh. Well, in that case,' Cori leaned reluctantly over her husband's form, 'we have to raise his head like this,' she slid a hand under the strong sinews of Greg's neck, lifting it slightly so that his mouth was raised at an angle to hers, 'and breathe air into his lungs like this.'

She bent so that her soft lips, cool from the water, covered the slackness of Greg's and felt his immediate masculine response in the tightening of his mouth, the raising of a large hand to encompass the small of her back to pull her down until her midriff met the steel wall of his chest. For a wild moment, Cori wished that she could stay there, the kiss deepening until it led to the inevitable conclusion, but Bobby's disgusted comment made her jerk her head away from Greg's, a shamed flush spreading under her tan.

'Aw, that's just like kissing,' Bobby stood back from them with his hands on his hips. 'How can you save somebody's life by kissing them?'

'You'd be surprised, Bobby,' Greg sat up in one fluid motion. His eyes went with a sardonic gleam to capture Cori's. 'The right kind of kiss has saved many a man's life.'

Cori pulled herself upright with a disgusted snort. 'We'll try again, Bobby, when we have a better patient,' she snapped, wheeling round on her heel to walk to the house, conscious of both Greg's and Marisa's eyes on the movement of her barely covered hips. One pair coolly appraising, she knew, the other narrowed in venom.

But she cared about neither pair of eyes, she told herself vehemently under the shower moments later. They were welcome to each other. The love she had felt for Greg was a tenuous thing, needing tender loving care to allow it to flourish to its fullness, and that nurturing would never come from the man who, by his own admission, had unbreakable ties with his brother's widow, whether or not he cared to acknowledge them by marrying her.

For his own reasons, he appeared to be keeping Marisa at arm's length for the time being ... to show his power over her? To prove that, even in a court of law, he could be triumphant? Yes, a man of his arrogance and need to dominate would go to those extreme lengths to assert his supremacy. Well, Marisa was welcome to taste the fruits of submission to the biggest male chauvinist of them all! For herself, Cori preferred a relationship where there was give as well as take, no one party taking precedence over the other.

CHAPTER NINE

'How long is Her Royal Highness staying this time?' Sherry asked in her laconic drawl the next morning at Jean Raeburn's house where several of the wives, including Cori, were having coffee.

'You mean Marisa?' Cori asked, startled by the dark girl's familiarity in referring to the woman she herself still held in a kind of awe because of her stature as a pianist.

'Who else? It must have been quite a traumatic blow to her to find you installed as Greg's wife! Wouldn't I have loved to see her face when he——'

'Cut it out, Sherry,' Jean interposed sharply, coming to refill Cori's cup from a large silver percolator, and seeming to speak more to Cori than to Sherry as she added: 'Greg's never been interested in Marisa Mason that way.'

'Oh?' Sherry returned snidely. 'And what about all those solitary rides they took every other time she's been here? Bob said——'

'Bob probably imagined Greg would do the same thing as he would if he was alone with a woman for any length of time,' Jean cut in scornfully, undisturbed by the brick red hue of anger that spread over Sherry's sallow skin.

'I've no idea how long she's staying,' Cori interposed hastily to avoid an outright argument, changing the subject by saying casually to Jean: 'I've been thinking about cutting my hair a lot shorter—would you do it for me?'

Jean had been a hairdresser before her marriage and was now official hairdresser to the ranch women—and men when occasion demanded—but now she stared aghast at Cori's long, thick hair. There was a chorus of protest from the other women, and Jean found her voice at last.

'Oh, Cori, you wouldn't do that—Greg would never let you, for one thing.'

Cori shrugged lightly. 'Oh, I don't think he'd mind one bit. He doesn't care what I do as long as I'm happy.' The first part of that statement was far more accurate than the last, she reflected wryly, knowing that Greg really didn't care about her in any other way than acting the part of his wife in a suitable manner.

'Well, I think you'll find that, like most men, Greg has a primitive streak in him about hair like yours! Must be a throwback to the days when they used to drag their women by the hair into their caves.'

The picture of Greg pulling her down by her hair to kiss her at the Anderson place flashed across Cori's mind and left her cheeks pink under the tan. She said no more then, but when she was leaving just before noon Jean called after her:

'Remember, I won't snip one snip unless I have Greg's handwritten permission! Even then I doubt if he'd speak to me again.'

Would Greg really care that much—or at all?—if her tresses were cut off? Perhaps in an abstract masculine way, but not in any personal sense. She was soon to find out, however, because Greg came from the enclosure that housed the bulls when she passed it, falling into step beside her to walk back to the house.

'You've been to a coffee party with the other wives?' he asked casually, taking off his hat to mop his brow that was wet with perspiration. Cori nodded, and he went on, giving her a sideways glance: 'You get on well with them, don't you?'

'As well as I need to,' she shrugged. 'It wouldn't be wise to develop close friendships here, would it?'

He walked a few steps in silence, then rammed his hat back on his head. 'No, I suppose not,' he said quietly. His eyes went up to the sky. 'We're in for a storm—a big one.'

'How do you know that?' she asked curiously, conscious only of the sticky heat that made his shirt stick to his back damply in places.

'That haze round the sun—the stillness everywhere— the quiet,' he answered in monosyllables that spoke more eloquently of his countryman's knowledge than a flowing speech by a weather expert could have done.

'That's true—I hadn't noticed,' she said, feeling the primordial quiet around them for the first time. She glanced up at his strongly carved features and down over the wide shoulders and broad back meant to carry the burdens of this rough country, and knew that there would always be Gregs to challenge it, bred from him and men like him, as he had been bred from the generations before him. This reminded her of Jean's remark about the primitive streak in him, and she said impulsively, not wanting to dwell on the thought of the woman who would bear his sons to carry on the line:

'I asked Jean to cut my hair short, but she——'

'You did *what*?'

He had halted his steps abruptly and was now staring down at her with eyes angrier than she had ever seen, his thick black brows lowered to furious points.

'I asked——'

'I heard you,' he interrupted with a sharp wave of his hand. 'And I forbid it! I'll tell Jean so myself when I see her.'

'What possible difference can it make to you whether my hair's short or long?' she demanded tartly, though her heart's beat had increased painfully at his obvious display of possessiveness. The beat regulated itself again when they stared into each other's eyes and she saw the anger fade slightly from his. Turning away, his shoulders betraying only a slight hunch of irritation, he started to walk again.

'None whatsoever,' he answered when she caught up with him on the hill. 'Your hair happens to be one of your best features, and I was speaking as any man might. But please yourself.'

With that she had to be content.

The storm developed as Greg had predicted, and as Cori helped Ellen prepare fruit pies for the freezer that afternoon, she heard the steady fall of rain outside, saw it blot out the distant mountains and surrounding hills and felt the volatile atmosphere in the house. Marisa snapped irritably at Bobby so that he fled to the kitchen for refuge, amusing himself for an hour with the pastry scraps Cori gave him but finally wandering up to his bedroom to get out the toys he had ignored while the weather was sunny and warm.

Marisa's restless fingers took up the notes of a Chopin Prelude on the piano, only to crash her fingers helplessly over the keys moments later.

Cori forgot that she herself would not be here to sample the wares intended to tide the Masons over the hard winter ahead. It was reward enough to know that she was part of a ritual that had gone on over the course of many years ... a woman attending to household necessities while her husband grappled with the more arduous chores out of doors.

'God!' Marisa exclaimed halfway through the afternoon when she came to the kitchen, her unsteady groping at the door for support evidence of her premature sampling of pre-dinner drinks. 'I'd forgotten how desolate this goddamn place can be at times! What are you doing, little wife-no-wife?'

Cori flushed, noting Ellen's puzzled expression as she came back from the sink with the fruit she had been cleaning.

'I'm making pies for the freezer,' she said coolly. 'Why don't you go back into the living room and I'll bring us some coffee?'

'Very worthy, aren't you?' Marisa sneered. 'But you won't get Greg that way, sweetie! He pays people to do ... that kind of thing.'

'Yes, I know,' said Cori, coming to put an arm round the slender figure, suppressing the involuntary thought that Marisa sounded exactly like Greg. As she shepherded the other woman out of the door, her lips formed the word 'coffee' and Ellen nodded understandingly, moving to the coffee pot beside the stove.

'And how much is he paying you to act the part of dear little wife?' Marisa asked insultingly when Cori straightened up from settling her in an armchair in the living room.

'Quite a lot!' Cori said waspishly, wishing yet shrinking from the thought that Greg could see his lady love at that moment.

Ellen said with a puzzled frown when she went back to the kitchen: 'What does she mean, you won't get Greg by making pies for him? You already have him ... he's your man and you're his woman. Till she came'—she jerked a derisive hand in the direction of the living room— 'Greg was happier than I ever saw him!'

Momentarily, Cori forgot the besotted woman in the other room. 'Was he, Ellen?' she asked wistfully.

'Sure he was. I'm not married, but I can tell when a man's found the woman he wants. That first night you came here, Greg told me he'd get fine sons from you ... you were his woman, he said.' Her dark eyes swept over Cori's slim figure. 'None yet, huh?'

'No,' Cori said hastily, turning in embarrassment to the coffee pot bubbling on the stove.

When Marisa had downed two cups of the strong black liquid, Cori left her and went to her room, turning from the dismal landscape outside the windows to stretch out on the wide marriage bed, her thoughts forming a pattern as she stared up at the ceiling. That Marisa Mason was the worst possible prospective wife for Greg was as clear as crystal ... to Cori, if not Greg. By no stretch of the imagination could she picture the lauded pianist as the wife of a rancher, content to spend her life complementing his in the remote outpost of Mason's Ridge.

But love seemed to strike in the most unlikely places, she told herself, and Marisa had made no pretence about her desire for Greg. If her word was to be trusted even John, her husband, had been aware of their passion for each others. Tears of compassion for John mingled with those she shed for her own hopeless love filled her eyes and ran down her cheeks. Damn Marisa ... and damn Greg for his allegiance to a woman who had far less to offer him than Cori herself had ...

Sounds of Greg showering in the bathroom brought Cori from a deep sleep filled with dreams, and she blinked as she looked round the room grown shadowy by the outside bleakness. The bathroom, when she entered it a short while later, still held the steam from Greg's shower and the towel he had impatiently discarded on the floor. Wife-like, she picked it up and stuffed it into the hamper before taking her own shower.

A half-resolved intention to prove her independence from a Greg who had made clear his preference for women in dresses prompted her to put on the coral pants suit she had worn at the Andersons'. His sister-in-law would more than fulfil his ideal of femininity, she told herself tartly, remembering the elegant creations Marisa assumed for the evening hours.

Her heart sank, however, as she walked noiselessly along the carpeted corridor to the living room. As on that other evening, conversation came clearly to her ears as she paused just beyond the archway, dismay bringing a frown between her brown eyebrows when she discerned that Marisa's voice was more befuddled than ever, signifying that she had stayed close to the bar instead of going to her room to change.

'... can't be such a fool as to think that ... girl ... could be convincing as your wife! Oh, Greg darling,' there was a pause as if Marisa had crossed the room. 'Send her away, and then there'll just be you and me, as it always ...'

'For God's sake, Marisa!' Greg's voice came explosively. 'Can't you think of somebody else for just a few minutes? What about Bobby?'

'I don't care about Bobby,' she cried passionately. 'I don't care if I never see him again, except that——'

Cori's head turned sharply to the stairs when an anguished gasp came from the upper level out of her view. Bobby! With Marisa's voice raised to that hysterical pitch, there could be no doubt that the boy had heard the wounding words. Cori's suspicions were confirmed when Bobby's jeans-clad figure ran swiftly down the stairs and disappeared to the back of the main hall where a door led to the outside.

In the few seconds Cori took to consider the wisdom of informing Greg and Marisa of the boy's flight, a time period that ended with her decision to pursue him herself —he wouldn't thank her if she raised a hue and cry only to be found sobbing in the garden area—Bobby had disappeared from the vicinity of the house.

Pondering again whether to inform the other adults, Cori mentally shrugged. She was wet already, and Bobby couldn't have gone far. Perhaps to one of his friends on the lower level. Slithering down the rain-slicked winding track from the house, Cori felt little cause for alarm. It was only when she reached the bottom and turned into the buildings area below that she heard the pound of reluctant hoofs on the soggy clay of the track and saw, in the gloomy half-light, the faint figures of boy and pony disappearing into the distance.

She paused at the stables and bit her lip in vexation. If only she had learned to ride as Greg had suggested several times! Rain splayed her hair flatly over her head and ran down her cheeks in rivulets while she stopped to think. As far as she knew, the beaten track Bobby had taken led only to the ranch houses, but from his frantic spurring of the pony, Cori had a suspicion that he had a further destination in mind.

Soaked, her hair plastered in wet strands to her head, her eyes fell on the machine shed opposite. She might not be able to ride a horse, but she could certainly drive the jeep and perhaps catch up with Bobby before he went too far across country unknown to her. Three minutes later she drove the jeep out of the shed, not stopping to close the big doors behind her.

Skidding from side to side, she passed corrals and barns and then the neat bungalows which already blazed with lights. Should she stop and ask one of the men for help?

But if she did that, Bobby could have gone too far away to be found that night, and the thought of the young boy exposed to the elements for any length of time forced Cori to press on, her streaming hands tightening whitely on the wheel as she left the track and hit what Greg had optimistically called 'the flat' of the valley to the rear of Mason's Ridge.

A movement up near the crest of an almost treeless hill at the far side of the river made her strain her eyes through the gloom. It was Bobby, but her heart sank. On horseback he had obviously been able to wade across the river, whereas she, with the jeep, was stuck on this side. Getting from the vehicle, she slithered across the rain-soaked grass to gaze down into the turbulent, mud-coloured waters below and knew it was hopeless to even consider wading through the swollen flow. Turning away with a despairing sob, knowing she would have to waste precious time in going back to the ranch for help, she stopped and stared disbelievingly at a dark outline spanning the river further downstream. A bridge!

It was built wide enough to accommodate a far larger vehicle, and the jeep went easily over the solid wood bridge; a minute later Cori was speeding as fast as the muddy ground permitted to the spot where she had seen Bobby, thankful that the hill slope was a gentle one. Only near the top did the engine protest, but in another moment they were over the crest, Cori skidding to a stop as yet another valley spread out before her. This one, though, appeared to be well clothed with trees and bushes down its centre, and as she watched for a sign of Bobby and the pony a flash of lightning over the distant mountains obligingly lit the area for a blinding second. Despair gripped Cori again when she saw the glint of water between the trees. Another river crossing! Would there be a bridge this time?

She set the jeep slowly into motion down the hill, for the first time feeling anger at Bobby's precipitate flight in weather like this. Then another streak of lightning jagged

across the sky and drove the anger from her. Coming at a
terrified pace from a gap in the bushes was Bobby's black
pony ... but no small figure sat astride the short-legged
animal's back. The lightning, Cori thought abstractedly.
Its suddenness must have startled the pony into bolting,
leaving Bobby—where?

Scarcely hearing the pounding hoofs as the pony veered
away from and past the jeep, Cori switched on the head-
lights and set off for the gap the animal had come from, fear
clamping her throat muscles to rigid hardness. Above the
noise of the engine she heard the rushing of deep flowing
water, and a moment later threw herself from the jeep to
peer frantically down a sharp incline leading to the river.

'Bobby? Bobby!' she shouted, fright making her voice
shrill. Her heart stopped beating for a sickening moment
when her eye caught sight of something white caught between the rocks at the far side of the river, recognising it
as Bobby's tee-shirt. 'Oh God!—Bobby!'

Without thought for her own safety, Cori slithered down
the bank and stepped into the water, feeling the immediate
strong tug at her calves and then at her knees as she
stumbled ahead over the mossily smooth and sharply
pointed rocks below the surface. Towards the centre the
rocks gave way to a deep void, and before Cori could even
cry out she was swept away like the bobbing tree trunk
that swirled beside her. Instinctively her hand went out
to grasp its sodden surface, then her arm slid across it to
anchor her more securely. Fear for Bobby overrode anxiety
on her own behalf and gave her a strength she was unaware
of possessing as she fought against the raging current and
aimed the log into the quieter eddy of water where Bobby
lay on his back moving gently up and down but showing no
signs of life.

Desperation lent power to her muscles, and she gasped
with relief when at last the trunk began to move outwards
from her pressure, shooting with speed towards half-sub-
merged rocks just below where Bobby lay, striking them
with a blow that jarred every bone in her body but which

led her into calmer waters where the current no longer tugged at her limbs. Taking no time to enjoy the blessed relief from the battering force, she half walked, half crawled, in the shallows to where Bobby lay.

A red graze across his forehead spoke eloquently as a reason for his unconscious state——he must have struck his head on the rocks when his pony threw him and bolted—— and she paused to collect her breath before bending her mouth to his in the lifesaving technique they had practised so unsuccessfully on Greg such a short time before.

Five minutes passed … ten … and cold crept through Cori until it seemed to reach her brain, numbing it into hallucinatory dreaminess as she worked with automatic rhythm over Bobby. A bed floated before her eyes … not a big bed, but one made warm because of the man's body beside her … warmth even in the burning glow of his black eyes as he pulled her down by the hair to kiss her … warmth in the lips that explored her eyes, her throat, her mouth …

'Cori?' a man's shout came. 'My God, Cori, are you all right?'

Dazedly her eyes took in the tall man's caped figure on a massive horse, and they seemed part of the dream she had been having. A faint gurgle from Bobby's throat brought her back to reality with a triumphant bump, and she called out to Greg as he began to lead his high-stepping horse across the river: 'Watch the middle, Greg—it disappears!'

Turning back to the spluttering Bobby, she cradled him in her stiff arms and waded towards the river bank, looking up numbly when Greg leaned down from the saddle to take the boy's light figure from her and hold out a hand to take hers, leading her firmly to shore.

'Put this round your shoulders,' he said, stripping off his rain cape and throwing it down to her, 'until I get back.'

'You're not leaving me here?' she cried, terror mingling with bone-deep cold to make her teeth chatter.

'Only for a few minutes, honey,' he said comfortingly. 'The cabin's not fifty yards from here ... I'll take Bobby and come back for you. Okay?'

Unable to speak, she nodded and lifted the heavy cape to settle it round her shoulders, feeling her way to a sizeable rock nearby and sitting on it while Greg negotiated the slope that was slightly less steep on this side of the river. She should have let him keep the cape to cover Bobby, she thought dully ... he had had more than enough water for one night.

Cori lost track of time as darkness closed in around her and fancies repossessed her mind. Had Greg really called her 'honey'? What would it be like to really be his honey, the sweetness that added spice to his life? The thought that had been uppermost in her mind while she was in the river now swept back into her mind. If she should drown here in this river, she would never know the fullness of Greg's love ... never experience his passion in the night, his waking beside her in the morning ...

Then like a half forgotten dream he was beside her, reaching down to pull her from the rock, his hands sliding under the cape as she lifted hers to lean against his sodden shirt-front for support. Like a second skin, the light material outlined the smooth muscles covering his chest and shoulders and exposed the dark shadow of short hairs below his neck. He had lost his hat somewhere along the way and, like Cori's, his hair was plastered close to his head.

Her arms went round to clamp his waist and her cheek settled against his chest, warm in spite of the wetness. 'Oh, Greg, I'm so glad you came! I thought I'd never see you again.'

The words which she would normally never have brought herself to say came from the deep exhaustion inside her, and she made no resistance when he removed one hand from under the cape to cup her chin with hard wet fingers, lifting it until she blinked at the rain falling full on her face.

'Cori!' he said once in a hoarse voice, then, as lightning

lit her upraised face, he groaned her name again and bent his head to hers, searching with hungry insistence for her lips and drawing all the remaining strength from her when he found them.

They were oblivious to the rain streaming down their faces and to the thunder rumbling through the mountains ... far greater was the thunder in Cori's mind and heart as her whole body suspended itself from Greg's fiercely encompassing mouth in the sure knowledge that this was where she belonged, this was where she was born to be. Nothing mattered apart from that—not Marisa's insinuations about John Mason's death, or her obvious desire for Greg. A desire that was not reciprocated, or Greg would not be kissing Cori as he was now with abandoned fervour as if the dam on his passions had finally given way.

Dizzy when he at last lifted his head to look searchingly at her before burying his face in her neck, she heard him mutter raggedly against her ear:

'I have to see to Bobby ... and you ... and light a fire.'

Cori jerked herself away. 'Bobby!' she gasped, stricken with guilt at having forgotten the boy who had been so near death.

'He'll be all right,' Greg assured her, his eyes going down to the hissing water round her feet. 'He brought up quite a lot of river water, but I've wrapped a blanket round him and he's in the dry.' He bent suddenly to pick Cori up as if she weighed nothing. 'You seem to have lost your shoes somewhere.'

'It doesn't matter,' she said huskily to his ear beside her mouth. 'Nothing matters ... now.'

Greg bore her easily up the short incline to where Ben, the magnificent chestnut stallion that was almost part of him, waited patiently, his back to the incessant rain. The horse's name had always struck Cori as prosaic for such a huge animal, his sleek flanks always seeming to glisten redly in the sun whenever she looked down towards the stables from the upper level. It was only when she saw him away from Greg that he seemed intimidating to her ...

together, they were a fluid team of perfect oneness.

Apparently sensing her reluctance to be put on the broad back, Greg continued to carry her in his arms towards the flickering, friendly light in the cabin window, a few quietly-spoken words to the horse sufficient to bring him docilely to walk just behind them.

At the door of the cabin, Cori insisted on being put down. 'Bobby might be scared if he sees you carrying me,' she explained. 'I wouldn't want him to think I'd been hurt because of——'

Greg's jaw tightened, but he set her down without a word and opened the door into the one-roomed cabin where Bobby sat shivering miserably on a hard-backed chair next to the table, a dark grey blanket clutched round him.

'You said you'd just be a minute, Uncle Greg,' he chat-tered accusingly. 'You've been gone a long time.'

His uncle merely grunted in reply and moved swiftly to the monstrous black stove on the far wall of the cabin, say-ing over his shoulder to Cori:

'Find yourself a blanket over there on the cot and put it round you while I get a fire started. You'll find a hook be-hind the door for the cape.'

Cori's teeth were also beginning to chatter as she took off the cape with stiff fingers and put it where he had in-dicated. 'It seems ... a shame to ... w-wet a blanket.'

'But do it,' he snapped irritably, turning from where he was hunched before the stove, his black brows and eyes unfriendly now as they went over her sodden pants suit clinging revealingly to her figure. 'It would be a greater shame if you get pneumonia!'

From the edged anger in his voice it seemed the last thing that would have worried him was the possibility of her falling ill, and tears smarted behind Cori's eyes as she went to the cot and picked up a similar blanket to Bobby's.

Why had he changed in such a short time? It was still only minutes ago when he had been kissing her passionately, abandonedly, making obvious his desire for her. Gulping back the sob in her throat, she padded across the floor to sit on another hard-backed chair near Bobby, her feet leaving wet imprints on the dusty floorboards.

The boy, too, sensed his uncle's angry mood and sat silently watching him at the stove, shivering occasionally, his dark hair standing in stiff spikes away from his troubled face.

At last the smell of burning wood permeated the small cabin, masking the faint musky odour Cori had noticed on entering it, and moment later yellow flames licked hungrily at the larger pieces of dry wood Greg had stacked behind the open bars. Soon there would be a red glow to throw life-giving heat into the room and its occupants, and she shivered anew in anticipation.

Finally satisfied, Greg stood up and glanced at his trembling nephew. 'Come on,' he said roughly, crossing the floor noisily in his tooled leather boots and lifting Bobby with one arm, taking the blanket from him as he set him on his feet by the roaring stove. Bobby was either too young or too subdued to be embarrassed by the stripping off of his wet clothes and being subjected to a brisk rubbing down with a well-worn towel Greg plucked from a makeshift cupboard beside the table. Even after the olive skin glowed with warmth, he continued to rub until Bobby said plaintively:

'You're taking my skin off, Uncle Greg!'

'I feel like taking the skin off your rear end, young man!' Greg returned grimly, but he stopped rubbing and in another moment had Bobby installed in the smaller of the two bunks ranged at an angle in the far corner of the room.

'Are you and Cori going to sleep in the other bunk?' he asked sleepily, eyeing the narrow cot doubtfully. 'You always say it's not big enough for you by yourself.'

'We'll manage,' Greg said briefly, turning back to where Cori still sat in a stupefied state near the fire. 'Now you,' he said with a briskness that snapped her out of her lethargy.

'I can manage myself, thanks,' she said hurriedly, sliding

the blanket from her shoulders and standing up.

A ghost of a smile hovered at the back of his eyes. 'I hadn't planned on giving you the same treatment as Bobby—though it might not be a bad idea, at that, after the ducking you just had.' His expression grew sober. 'I'm —grateful for what you did for Bobby. I'm sure his mother will be too.'

Cori gasped, forgetting the damp cling of her clothes. 'His mother! She must be worried sick about him!'

'She won't be,' he replied nonchalantly, moving to the door and taking down the rain cape. 'I guessed Bobby would head towards the cabin and that you'd follow him here. I told Hank to tell Marisa not to worry if we didn't come back tonight.'

Would she have worried anyway? From her previous remarks, Marisa could hardly be considered a natural mother, with the concern that implied.

'I'm going out to see to the horse,' said Greg, picking up the hat he had left near the door. 'By the time I get back you should be finished changing. You might find the bedspread over there a little less bulky than a blanket to wrap round you.' He indicated the cotton homespun spread on the other bunk and went out, closing the door quickly against the gust of rain that met him.

A quick glance over at Bobby after the door closed assured Cori that the boy was asleep, and she stripped off the wet pants suit and soaked underwear, giving herself a cursory rub down with a fresh towel before wrapping the gold spread round under her arms and securing it with a tuck in at the hollow between her breasts. She had pulled one of the hard chairs over nearer the fire and was towelling her hair dry when Greg came back in with a suddenness that startled her.

Water drops splashed from his hat as he shook it and hung it behind the door, following it with the glistening rain cape that dripped heavily on the dusty floor below. His hair, already partially dry, fell over his brow and gleamed with blue-black dampness as he came towards her and took up a stance beside her with his back to the stove. Steam rose from his clothes and Cori exclaimed: 'Greg, you're steaming! You should take off those wet things.'

'Do I detect wifely concern?' he mocked, but his fingers went to the buttons on his shirt and he stripped it away from his damp torso with an impatient movement, letting it fall on the table nearby. His hands dropped to the snake-buckle belt round his pants and Cori half turned away from him, letting her drying hair fall like a curtain between them to afford him privacy.

'You can turn back now—I'm decent,' he said moments later, and she saw that though he had draped one of the towels round his middle, it did little to hide the smoothly taut muscles of his thighs. 'Would you like some coffee?'

Cori looked at him in amazement. '*Coffee?* Here? You shouldn't joke about such things.'

'No joke. I keep some supplies up here, and I brought some water in with me after I saw to Ben.'

'I can't think of anything in the world I'd rather have right now than a cup of coffee.'

'It'll be black.' he warned as he padded barefoot to the door and came back with an enamel jug which he placed on top of the stove before taking a can of coffee from one of the cupboards. He paused there, taking stock of its contents, then said: 'Are you hungry?'

'Starved! Don't tell me you have food there too?'

'I can offer you baked beans ... or baked beans ... or——'

'I'll settle for the baked beans, I think,' she said, as if he had offered her an extensive menu, and got to her feet. 'Let me see to the coffee while you do the beans.'

She stepped towards him, forgetting the trailing hem of the bedspread, and stumbled as her foot caught in the folds, dragging her carefully contrived tuck-in apart but leaving her no time for embarrassment as she pitched towards the stove. Greg's arm flashed out and swung her round, pulling her with an instinctive movement against him, his tough-skinned hands rough against the silky skin of her hips. The leap of desire in his eyes was echoed in her own suddenly snatched breath as she became aware of her softness crushed to his chest, the hardened thrust of his thighs against her, the suddenly uneven breath from his widened nostrils that felt warm on her face.

'Greg?' she whispered in mute question, and felt his head bend towards her, one hand rising to spread seeking fingers through the hair he hadn't wanted cut off. Just as her lips parted softly to receive his kiss, Bobby moved restlessly on his cot and cried out in his sleep.

The tension went out of Greg immediately, his eyes going from hers to the sleeping boy before he bent with an angry exclamation to pick up the fallen bedspread and drape it round her with savage tightness.

'You'd better sit down,' he said harshly. 'I'll see to things.'

Despite his anger, and his avoidance of her eyes as he threw coffee into the jug on the stove, joy coursed through Cori in the knowledge that, had it not been for Bobby's presence in the cabin, their marriage would have become real that night. The reality would perhaps have been different for each of them—to her, the fulfilment of every romantic dream she had ever had; to him, the physical satisfaction of union with a woman attractive to him. But surely, from the tenuous bonds of a physical coming together the tendrils of a more spiritual togetherness might take root and flourish?

Looking across at his ruffled black hair and broad muscled back, she knew that she wanted Greg's love in whatever form it came—physical, spiritual, or a fusion of the two.

CHAPTER TEN

CORI woke as early light filtered greyly in at the small square window over the table, wondering where she was until she heard the murmur of voices close by.

'I'm sorry, Uncle Greg,' Bobby was saying penitently. 'I didn't know it would make so much trouble for everybody when I ... when I ran away.'

'Sure you didn't, son,' Greg replied in a tender voice Cori had never heard from him before. 'But you could have got Cori killed as well as yourself by your foolish action.'

'I'd never want to do that,' Bobby gulped, pausing before going on: 'You love Cori a lot, don't you, Uncle Greg?'

A long silence ensued, then Greg's feet scraped on the floor as he rose. 'Don't worry any more about it. You're both safe, that's all that matters.'

'Uncle Greg?'

'Mmm?'

'Mommy said ...' Bobby's words trailed away and Greg put in tersely:

'Your mother says a lot of things she doesn't mean, Bobby. She was—upset last night about something else. She didn't mean what you heard her say.'

'Oh.' Bobby seemed to digest this. 'Did she mean it when she said I'd go with her next time she leaves the Ridge?'

'Do you want to?'

'No! I want to stay with you ... and Cori.'

'Then you'll stay. Now be quiet or you'll wake Cori before I've got the coffee ready.'

Bobby stifled a giggle. 'You sure didn't sleep very late in that bunk, did you?'

'No. Like you said, there's not much room there.'

Cori kept her eyes closed as his booted feet went less noisily than usual to the stove. Why hadn't he told Bobby that he had slept on the floor in a sleeping bag he had unearthed from one corner of the cabin? The thought occupied her for several minutes until the delicious aroma of freshly perked coffee wafted through the room and drove everything else from her mind. She peeped through her lashes and saw Greg bent over the stove taking the coffee pot from it, a towel wrapped round his hand against the heat. He was fully dressed again, his blue jeans stretched tightly across flat stomach and hips, taut over powerfully formed thighs and long legs, no creases showing anywhere apart from the slightly crumpled appearance of his light plaid shirt.

Cori's eyes fell on her own clothing spread on chairs close to the fire to dry, pants suit on one, underwear on the other, and an embarrassed flush crept into her cheeks as Greg came towards her with a steaming cup. He must have set her clothes out to dry after she had gone to bed; she had been too conscious of his masculine presence to do more than heap her things on the back of one chair.

'Has—has the rain stopped?' she stammered, sitting up on one elbow and clutching the grey blankets round her as she took the cup from his hand, thanking him with a trembling smile.

'Pretty well. I'm going down now to check on the jeep ... if it's okay, we should all be able to get away together.'

Her softly curling brown lashes swept up as she looked at him. 'And if it isn't?'

He shrugged. 'Then I'll have to take one of you on Ben and come back for the other.' He called to Bobby, who was watching them with bright eyes. 'Come on, sport—up you get! You can come down to check the jeep with me, then Cori can get dressed in peace.'

Bobby, evidently not suffering much from his experience of the evening before and seeming shyer now than he had been last night, hopped past Cori on his way to the stove. clutching one of the blankets to him.

'Hi, Cori,' he said, giving her a diffident smile. 'Are you okay?'

'I'm fine, Bobby. How about you?'

'Okay too, I guess.' His dark eyes were solemn suddenly. 'I'm sorry, Cori, I didn't mean—I didn't think——'

'Don't worry about it, honey,' Cori cut in softly. 'Just don't ever forget that there are people who love you a whole lot. People who would be very unhappy if anything happened to you.'

For a moment Bobby's lips quivered as if he was on the verge of tears, but Greg's purposely gruff: 'Hurry up, son!' sent him scurrying over to his uncle with nothing more than a few blinks of his dark lashes. How alike they were, Cori mused as the tall man bent over the boy in helping him to dress. Greg's son would look very like Bobby, she thought, discreetly turning her head away and sipping her coffee. Sturdy but vulnerable in the as yet spindly turn of elbow and knee, hair like the raven's wing, though Bobby's had a slightly lighter hue ...

Greg's sons ... the possibility that she herself might become their mother had seemed less remote last night than any other time. Her eyes grew dreamy at the thought and she hardly heard Greg's quietly spoken:

'We won't be long, Cori.' He walked with Bobby to the door, one hand loosely yet possessively on the slight shoulder.

'All right, Greg,' she said with such soft huskiness that his black eyes turned to look questioningly at her. Hastily, she added: 'I'm just getting up,' and followed the words with action as soon as the door closed behind them. As she pulled on the clothes warmed by the stove, her mind veered back to the evening before and her eyes grew soft as they went round the simple cabin's interior.

Of all the places in the world to begin her real marriage to Greg Mason, none could be more perfect than this one. The stark simplicity of the cabin's interior, the ruggedly isolated country beyond its window, all breathed of the man himself and made him one with their primitive force.

She was thoughtful as she folded up the blankets and pushed back the chairs to their former positions, her eyes flying to the frown between Greg's brows when he and

Bobby stamped back in a few minutes later.

'The jeep's stuck fast in a gully,' he told her tersely. 'I'll need help to get it out. Will you mind staying here while I take Bobby back to the ranch?'

'No ... no, of course not. I'm—sorry about the jeep, Greg.'

His voice seemed curt. 'It wasn't your fault. The rain softened the ground so that it slid back down into the gully—we're lucky it didn't go the other way into the river.' He opened the door again and Cori saw that Ben had been brought round ready for their departure. 'Up you go, Bobby!'

He swung the boy up into the saddle and turned back to look at Cori. 'I shouldn't be long. There's plenty of wood to keep the fire going, and I've put a supply of water out here in case you need more coffee.' A lightning smile lit his features. 'There's also more beans if you feel inclined to eat.' For a brief moment it seemed he was about to add something else, then he turned back to the horse.

'Greg?'

'Mmm?'

Cori's heart pounded and she licked lips that were suddenly dry. 'When—when you come back ... will you stay?'

His head snapped round and angled so that his eyes looked directly, searchingly, into the clear hazel of hers, reflecting a dozen different emotions in as many seconds. His face moved slightly away from her when a soft snicker came from the horse behind him.

'Take Ben for a walk,' he commanded Bobby tightly. 'I want to talk to Cori for a minute.'

'Aw, Uncle Greg, that means kissing and stuff, and Ben doesn't like me much,' Bobby protested. 'What if he throws me?'

'He won't throw you,' Greg returned unsympathetically. 'Now do as I say.'

A slight pat of his hand on the chestnut rump sent the slender legs into motion, and Greg came back into the cabin, almost closing the door but keeping one hand on the latch. Cori blinked nervously when his eyes captured hers again.

'Do you mean what I think you mean?'

'Yes.' The word came as a faint sigh through her quivering lips and his eyes narrowed in concentration on her face.

'You want to make this marriage ... a real one? Here?' His eyes lifted to sweep round the room before returning to hers with hard enquiry.

This time she could only nod, dropping her head and turning it slightly so that her hair partially obscured her expression. The shield was effective for only a moment, however, because Greg stepped forward and lifted her chin with chilly fingers, his voice no warmer when he ground out:

'And what would make it different this time from the last occasion we were in bed together? Would you grit your teeth to stop yourself from crying for another man when I touched you?'

Cori gasped and wrenched her chin away from his hand, her eyes wide pools of disbelief. He had thought, that night at the Andersons', that her tears were for Roger! Her voice trembled when she denied: 'I wasn't crying because of Roger, I——'

'No? Then maybe you'd explain what the tears were for! I'll admit it was a new experience for me to have a woman cry when I made love to her—and if she ever wished I was someone else, she hid it a lot better than you were able to!'

Humiliation rolled over her in a painful wave and brought the sharp sting of tears to her eyes. How could she have misconstrued his actions the night before? Every cell in her body had been aware of his desire for her, the abandonment of control at the river when his kisses were wild with sweetly savage possessiveness.

Her tongue groped for words to tell him that Roger had been far from her thoughts that night in the Andersons' small guest room. Yet how could she do that without also letting him know that it was Marisa, the woman he had been dreaming about, that he made love to?—not Cori, his pretend wife who happened to be handy.

Her hand lifted in a helpless little gesture that did nothing to soften the harsh lines round his mouth. 'It—it wasn't the way you think. Anyway, it doesn't matter now. Roger's engaged to——'

'Oh, I see,' he cut in, sarcasm edging the understanding softness of his tone. 'So you thought you'd transfer your romantic notions to me on the strength of what happened down there last night.' His head jerked towards the door, then he went on with mocking cruelty: 'I hate to disillusion you, but that little incident was a show of gratitude, nothing more. I'm a physical man, and I express myself accordingly.'

Cori's breath was knocked from her body as if he had struck her, tears forgotten as her eyes widened on his immovably strong face. It would have given her great satisfaction to rip that confident male expression from his face with her finger nails, but even as the furious thought formed it died away. His air of lethargy covered, she knew, an animal-like swiftness when occasion demanded, and he would not stand idly by while she extracted her revenge.

'Gratitude?' she choked at last. 'For what?'

'For saving Bobby's life, of course.' His brows rose in assumed surprise. 'You were—very brave to do what you did. Naturally, I——'

'You can save your gratitude for someone who appreciates it!' Cori snapped, anger making her eyes sparkle dangerously. 'And I'd be glad if you'd forget my—my offer. You're not the only one who shows gratitude in a physical way!'

His jaw tensed, then relaxed as a flame glowed deep in his eyes. 'You turn me on a lot more when you're fighting me like this than when you offer yourself on a platter,' he said softly, amused.

'You're hateful!' Cori threw back impotently, her voice trembling with rage and an emotion she could not assess at that moment. 'Don't bother to come back for me—I'll walk.'

'Without shoes?' His eyes went down to her stockinged feet. 'You'd find it sticky going.'

'I'd prefer sinking over my head in mud to riding on that —that *beast* with you!'

'Uncle Greg?' Bobby's shrill voice came from beyond the partially opened door.

'Coming, Bobby,' Greg raised his voice to say as he turned away from Cori.

'Hank's here with some of the men!' the boy shouted excitedly above Ben's alert whinnies.

Greg paused with his hand on the door and looked back tormentingly at Cori. 'Maybe you'd rather ride with Hank, and I know he'd be thrilled if you did.' But when Cori began to say she would be glad to go with anyone provided it wasn't him, he cut her off with a sorrowful shake of his head: 'Too bad I can't let you do that. It wouldn't look right for my wife to hold on to another man that closely.'

'That won't matter one bit after I tell them you've called me your wife for the last time!' she threw after him with barbed sweetness, but he did no more than check his stride momentarily before going on to meet the men who had come searching for them.

Cori paced the cabin floor restlessly after Greg left it to go with the men down to the river. Occasionally she stepped over to the open door to peer out in the direction from which the male voices floated back to her, eventually hearing the coughing start of the jeep's engine, triumphant relief surging through her when she realised the significance of that sound. Now there would be no need for her to ride behind Greg on that massive horse of his! So exultant was she that she contemplated traversing the distance between cabin and river on foot, but a glance at the inches-deep mudprints left by Ben's hoofs changed her mind. She could stand a ride on the stallion's back as far as the jeep, she decided, even if it meant sitting behind Greg.

She had resumed her pacing when the final roar of the jeep's resurrection reached her and grew fainter again as it

—*moved away*? Racing to the door, she cursed the trees
and bushes that hid her view of the river area. But there
could be no doubt that the jeep was being driven back to the
ranch without her. Soon there was not even the echo of
its high-pitched engine, and the silence seemed even more
profound as she considered the possibility that she had
been left behind ... deliberately ...

But what had Greg told Bobby and the other men? That
she loved the cabin so much she wanted to spend more
time there? That he would be coming back with supplies
for at least another night in the isolated hideout? This last
thought made her breath catch noisily in her throat. What
had he said?

'You turn me on a lot more when you're fighting me like
this when you offer yourself on a platter.'

'No way, Greg Mason,' she muttered half aloud. The man
she had loved and wanted a matter of hours ago was now
just as hated and despised. She would be gone from the
cabin by the time he returned, taking a circular route back
to the ranch and, if she was lucky, have enough time to
phone the charter company which had supplied Marisa's
plane. And when the plane arrived to take her away, even
Greg would not risk a scene, so letting the outside world
know about his marriage of convenience. The most liberal
court in the land would hardly look on a man who would go
to such extremes as a fit guardian for a young boy. Bobby
himself she thrust from her mind. She had come to love
him, but surely his place was with his mother, who might
make more of an effort if Cori was out of the picture.

Feeling more optimistic, she looked again at the oozing
grassland before her, then up to the rain-washed sky where
a sun with little warmth in it was struggling for supremacy
with thinning clouds. Despair engulfed her again, knowing
that the ground would take hours—perhaps days—to dry
out, and Greg, who knew this land like the back of his
hand, would easily be able to follow her progress over the
soggy terrain.

Her back touched the door-frame as she slid to the

ground and leaned her head on her upraised knees, giving vent to the tears that had been building up all that emotional morning. To go from warm contemplation of the deepest commitment she could make to Greg, to shocked recognition of his sardonic rejection was more than her weakened state could bear. But worst of all was the realisation that however badly he had treated her, Greg would always be the only man who could touch the right chords in her heart, make her woman's body ache with wordless longing. Hatred born of hurt had clouded her vision momentarily, but the thought of leaving Mason's Ridge and never seeing Greg again was like a knife wound in her breast.

It was when her shoulders had stopped shaking in a paroxysm of delayed reaction that she sensed a presence beside her. Raising her head slightly from the arms cradling it, she saw four slender chestnut legs cuffed with muddy white a few yards away and, further up, a man's leather-booted foot thrust into a stirrup.

'Cori? Why are you crying?'

Greg swung himself down from the saddle and threw the reins distractedly over Ben's back, his hands surprisingly gentle as he raised Cori to her feet.

'I—I thought you'd—left me,' she murmured with the utter dejection of a child, and felt her chin being lifted up so that her eyes met the searching enquiry of Greg's. Not even the knowledge that she looked her worst, her cheeks moist with tears, her uncombed hair falling in an unruly mass past her shoulders, could spark even a little life into her listless body.

'You know I wouldn't have done that,' he said gently, feeling in his pocket for the handkerchief which, when he produced it, was clean but crumpled. Without offering it to her, he dabbed at her cheeks and eyes himself, then submitted her to the indignity of having her nose blown. It was the humiliation of this act that brought a light back to her tear-stained eyes.

'How could I know that?' she demanded, gulping noisily as she caught a hiccup in her throat. 'You said—all those

-horrible things, and—you didn't c-come back when—the jeep left . . .' Her voice trickled away as fresh tears filled her eyes.

'I didn't come back right away because I needed time to think—as well as going to look for your shoes.' His eyes grew darker, a feat she would not have thought possible. 'I know what it was you were offering me, Cori, and believe it or not, that's what I've wanted from the minute I laid eyes on you at Howard's party.'

Shock stopped her tears in their tracks and her breath drew inward on an audible note. What was he saying? He had wanted her for his real wife from the beginning? But . . .

'Y-you've never given any . . . s-sign . . .' she gasped, her brain whirling dizzily so that she swayed towards the solid breadth of his chest and felt his arms go round her waist to support her.

'Haven't I?' he asked softly, then his eyes grew bleak. 'There was a night—or early morning—at Bill's when I thought you might have come to think of me in the same way as . . .' His arms tightened round her. 'But when I looked at you and found you crying because I wasn't—*Roger*——' he spat out the name as if he hated the feel of it on his lips.

'But I told you this morning it wasn't Roger I was crying about,' she cried. 'I've hardly given him a thought since I—came here.'

'Is that the truth?' His fingers caught in the silk strands of her hair, pulling her head back so that his eyes had free access to her face. He seemed satisfied then that she had spoken the truth, but persisted:

'Then why were you crying if it wasn't for him?' The heavy black line of his brows drew down. 'Were you afraid of me?—of how I felt about you?'

'No!' The cry was spontaneous, born as it was from the remembrance that she had discovered her love for him in those moments at the Andersons', and that she would have become his wife then had it not been for—'I was—crying —because I thought you were making love to—another woman. The one you were dreaming about when I woke you.'

He gave an anguished groan. 'Cori, you couldn't be more wrong. Believe me, I knew exactly what I was doing—and who you were.' The tone of his voice changed abruptly, his frown deepening the ridge between his eyes. 'What made you believe I was thinking of another woman?'

Her eyes glanced off his, then dropped away. In a low voice, she said: 'You called out for—Marisa—begging her ...'

'*Marisa?*' he queried with heartening incredulity. 'You thought that I——? Oh, Cori, the only reason I can think of that I'd be dreaming about—begging something from —Marisa is that she'd let me have Bobby so that I could bring him up the way his father wanted!'

'Oh, Greg ... Greg,' she sighed, her arms creeping up over his shirt front to clasp round the strong arch of his neck, 'I thought——'

'I think you've—we've *both* been thinking the wrong things for too long,' he returned with husky gentleness, his fingers tightening in her hair to pull her face up to meet his descending mouth. Like the lightning of the previous evening, his lips sent illuminating flashes along her nerves as they touched her lids in turn, her cheeks, and along the line of her jaw until they settled more permanently on her mouth, parting her lips easily to woo her with an expertness that sent shockwaves of ecstasy through her veins.

She shivered when his hands ran over the silky material of her top to her hips, holding there for long moments to press her yielding body to the aggressive hardness of his before sliding up under the top to sweep abrasively over her skin until she moaned sighingly against his mouth.

'Does that offer still hold good?' he asked in a ragged whisper, hardly waiting for her speechless nod before lifting her effortlessly in his arms and sealing her lips with his again as he carried her into the cabin, his booted heel catching the door to slam it shut ...

CHAPTER ELEVEN

ONCE over the still-bubbling river, Cori relaxed against Greg's chest, feeling Ben's movements beneath her as a soothing background to the contentment that filled her being. A contentment that stemmed from the joyous knowledge of her womanhood, her ability to move and satisfy the deep-felt hungers of the man whose arms now circled her protectively as his bronzed hand held the reins that guided the horse home. That his hunger took more than one form she was made aware of a moment or two later when he put his lips to her ear and groaned:

'I'm so famished I could even eat one of Ellen's meals with relish!'

Cori turned to give him a glancing smile. 'You always eat everything she prepares anyway.'

'Only because I don't want to hurt her feelings—and because I get hungry working in the air all day.' His jaw nuzzled her cheek, reddening it where the unshaven bristles scratched her more tender skin. 'Somehow, I feel Ellen won't be able to satisfy my needs from now on. You're a much better—cook than she is.'

'Oh?' she asked with a pert lift of her brows. 'That's the only difference between Ellen and me?'

He seemed to give maddening consideration to the question before answering slowly: 'Well, her hair doesn't have a band of gold round it where the sun strikes it when she sits at the dining room table ... her figure isn't one that would put most Hollywood stars to shame ... and her eyes aren't like a beautiful book I hate to stop reading.'

'For an unromantic man, you say the nicest things,' Cori said unsteadily as she turned to kiss the hardened stubble of his jaw, only to find her lips imprisoned and held in the fierce possession of his.

A long time later Ben snorted as if to warn them that they were approaching the bridge leading to the ranch buildings, and Cori pulled her face away, laughing breathlessly. 'I don't think Ben approves of these goings-on on his back!'

'I'll remind him of that next time I bring a fetching filly for his pleasure!' Greg chuckled, straightening as they crossed the bridge and the first houses came up on their left. Pique stabbed Cori when she realised that Greg had no intention of sharing their new-found happiness with anyone on the ranch, least of all the employees who had accepted their marriage as real from the beginning. Love to Greg would always be a private thing, a precious part of his life conducted far away from the prying eyes of others. A love that would blossom and grow in the Shangri-la he had built halfway to the Ridge, in the master bedroom he would now share with her.

'Hi there!' Hank's cheerful voice came from the calf pen they were passing, and he grinned up at them as he leaned on the fence. 'I was about to head up a search party to come and find you.'

'Just as well for your sake that you didn't!' Greg retorted equably, reining Ben in while he stopped to pass a few words with the foreman.

Cori's cheeks had coloured when Hank's knowing smile encompassed herself as well as Greg, but she recognised as the two men chatted that in this untamed country a man with a fairly recent wife was regarded as much with envy as ribald derision.

Ben carried them all the way up to the gravelled entrance before the house and Greg, mindful of the sharp-edged stones, carried Cori in his arms to the porch, where he set her on her feet and bent his head to kiss her with promising precision.

'Much as I want you,' he murmured with warm breath against her ear, 'I'd be grateful if you could rustle us up a couple of steaks first.'

'Cupboard lover!' she laughed, detaching herself from him. 'But as the thought of a slightly underdone steak surrounded with mushrooms done in butter appeals a lot more at this moment than your unshaven chin, I'll comply.'

He positively drooled. 'I don't know if I'll be able to hold out till I get back.' Seeing her puzzled expression, he explained: 'I have to take Ben down and get him settled, then see to a few other things. By that time, you should have the meal ready.'

Fearlessly, Cori put her hand on the smooth neck of the horse that had carried them home. 'Thank you, Ben. You've restored my faith in horse nature!'

'You'll have to learn to ride now, Cori.' Greg said urgently, one hand going to grasp the reins before he swung lightly into the saddle and looked down at her. 'I want you to come with me as much as possible.'

His 'now' pointed up more than anything else could have the change in their relationship, and there was an answering shine in her eyes when she said:

'I will, Greg. I'll learn how to ride and come out with you every chance I get!'

Her insides melted with pleasure as he led Ben back to the downward trail and raised a hand in salute before he disappeared down it. Money didn't bring happiness, she sighed, turning back to the house—neither did material possessions or the extraneous fripperies of society. All that was important was the love of two people for each other.

Ellen's worried face met her in the hall. 'Oh, I'm so glad to see you back, Cori,' she said with heartfelt relief, her eyes turning with an almost frightened watchfulness to the stairs behind her. 'Mrs Mason's been behaving in a funny way ever since Bobby got back. She's been drinking that stuff'
-the housekeeper's head went with a jerk to the drinks cabinet in the living room—'and she's been trying to get a plane to take her out of here. She says she's going to——'

'*Cori!* Cori, you tell Mommy I don't have to go!' Bobby had flown down the stairs and buried his dark head against her waist. 'Uncle Greg said I could stay here with you and him!'

'Bobby, get yourself together and tell me what's going on here.' Cori disengaged the slight body from her and looked into his apprehensive eyes.

'Mommy—says she's going to—take me away from here,' the boy sobbed, his arms going round Cori as if she was a lifeline. 'I don't want to go to—New York and—London and all the places she's talking about! Please, Cori!'

'It's all right, Bobby,' she soothed, though her eyes above his head were troubled. 'If Uncle Greg said you can stay, then you'll stay.'

'Is Greg coming soon?' Ellen voiced her own heartfelt wish.

'Yes, he has a few things to attend to down below,' Cori answered automatically, then, remembering her promise of a steak, she said: 'Take a couple of steaks from the freezer, Ellen, will you? And mushrooms—we have some frozen, haven't we?'

'Yes—yes, I think so,' the housekeeper replied, seeming glad of concise orders of what to do. 'But Mrs Mason——'

. 'I'll talk to her,' Cori said with more confidence than she was feeling. 'Take Bobby into the kitchen with you while I'm upstairs.'

She hesitated at the foot of the stairs, then went up to face the woman who held Greg's peace of mind in her hands. His brother had wanted Bobby to be brought up here at Mason's Ridge, far away from the itinerant life Marisa could give him, and as Greg's wife Cori knew that she was with him all the way. To persuade Marisa that Bobby would be better off at Mason's Ridge was another matter entirely.

Wishing that she had taken time to at least brush her hair, Cori knocked at Marisa's door and went in, blinking at the sight of suitcases and mounds of clothing piled on every available surface in the room. Marisa stood in the middle of it, her slender but voluptuous figure still dressed in a black negligée which revealed considerably more than it concealed.

'Marisa, I think—that is, *Greg* and I think——'

'Greg and you!' Marisa laughed contemptuously. 'You think because he's slept with you once he's yours for life!

Well, let me tell you, my dear, that doesn't mean a thing to Greg Mason!' The tranquil look was gone as the dark woman's mouth twisted into an ugly line. 'You wouldn't know what to do with a man like Greg Mason if he was handed to you in a package tied with blue ribbon marked "press here" and "open this end",' she spat vindictively.

'I managed pretty well this morning,' Cori was stung into replying as she advanced into the room. 'But I didn't come here to talk about that. I want to speak to you about Bobby.'

'Bobby?' Marisa's vague tone indicated her thoughts were elsewhere. 'What do you mean, "this morning?" Bobby told me you and Greg spent the night in that little bunk up at the cabin.'

Of course, Cori thought. Bobby had asked Greg if he was going to sleep there, and Greg had said they'd manage. Added to that was the fact that he hadn't told Bobby that his bed had been a sleeping bag by the fire . . .

A faint tap on the door indicated Ellen's arrival with a pot of coffee and cups on a tray, and Cori blessed her with her eyes, if only because of the extra time it gave her to prepare her plea for Bobby.

'Drink this,' she said after pouring a cup of the dark brew and handing it to Marisa. 'You'll feel better.'

'Feel better? What do you know about how I feel?' Although she made no attempt to drink the coffee, Marisa held it fiercely in her hands. 'Oh, you're all bright and bushy-tailed because Greg's made love to you at last—I know the signs. But how will you feel when he throws you over for somebody younger, as I've been pushed aside for you?'

Cori's heart began to beat like a sledgehammer, and to cover her agitation she poured coffee for herself and sipped the scalding brew unthinkingly. Greg would have told her, when she faced him with the fact that it was Marisa he had been dreaming about that night, if there had been anything between himself and the dark-haired pianist. His incredulous denial had rung clearly with truth.

'Come off it, Marisa,' she said with stinging contempt.

'There was never anything between you and Greg—except what was dreamed up in your own mind!'

'He told you that?'

'He didn't have to,' Cori returned quietly. 'He's not the kind of man who would——'

'What do you know about the kind of man he is?' Marisa cried hysterically, the calm look of the Madonna completely gone from her ravaged face. 'Do you really believe he would tell you how he killed his brother to get him out of the way? And that he got an attack of conscience after it and wouldn't touch me again?'

Cori rose stiffly. 'You're sick, Marisa. Greg could never do a thing like that for any woman, no matter how much he—cared for her.'

The dark eyes flared angrily, then narrowed to little more than slits. 'For a woman—perhaps not. For his son—definitely yes!'

Marisa gave a crowing laugh when Cori's face registered first shock, then disbelief. 'Why do you think Greg's so anxious to keep Bobby with him? Because he's his dead brother's child? Hardly!'

'Bobby is ... Greg's son?' Cori whispered, her mouth suddenly dry as she faced the taunting cruelty of the other woman's smile. 'I don't believe you!'

'Work it out for yourself. You must have seen Bobby's picture of John and me—didn't it strike you as odd that he was so fair while Greg is so—dark?'

The room rocked around Cori and she groped for a handhold on the dresser behind her. Visions rose before her eyes—her own thoughts on first seeing Bobby with Greg, that the boy could almost be his ... son!—having to ask Bobby the first time she went to his room who the fair-haired man in the picture was—only this morning reflecting as Greg dressed the boy, how alike they were—Greg's obsession with keeping Bobby with him ...

She mumbled something incoherent and stumbled from the room, wanting only to get away from the mockingly triumphant look in Marisa's eyes.

Reaching the master bedroom without knowing how she got there, and not seeing the neatly made wide bed—the bed she had thought would be shared with Greg from that night forward—she staggered to the red-upholstered chair by the window and huddled into it, her eyes staring sightlessly over the wide landscape of hills and valleys. Hunger had gone from her as well as every other bodily need. She had planned on taking a hot bath on their return, changing into a dress that would reflect her happiness and draw admiration from Greg's eyes, and using the perfume she had been saving for such a special occasion. But none of these things entered her mind now as she sat in frozen immobility hugging her arms, which had suddenly become cool to her touch.

She had no idea of time passing, only lifting her head dully to look across to the door as the handle rattled and Greg's voice came from the other side.

'Cori? Let me in, I have to talk to you.'

Had he seen Marisa and been told that Cori knew the truth of what he had hidden from her? Her empty stomach shrank at the thought of facing him, and perhaps hearing more lies in justification, but she went across to the door nonetheless and turned the lock.

His eyes held a suppressed air of excitement when he came into the room, and he seemed not to notice her washed out expression.

'Cori, I have to fly up to the logging section right away. The foreman just contacted us on the radio—some of the men have come down with food poisoning, and they might need hospital care, so I'm taking Hank along too. Nobody's in a fit state to fly their plane, so Hank and I will have to manage between us.'

'You haven't eaten,' she said automatically.

'I've told Ellen to rustle something up in a hurry.' His voice softened and lowered. 'Those steaks smothered in mushrooms will have to wait a day or two till I get back.'

'A—day or two?'

Misunderstanding her meaning, he put sinewy arms

round her to draw her close and said against her ear: 'I'd planned other things for tonight, but we'll make up for it when I get back. I'm taking some of my men up to the camp and we'll all have to pitch in so that the contract goes according to schedule.' His mouth came round to cover hers then, but after a moment or two he raised his head to look enquiringly into her eyes. 'What's wrong, honey? Changed your mind about me already?'

'No—no, I—I'm just tired, that's all,' she said, dropping her eyes and moving out of his hold.

'And hungry, too. Ellen's making enough for both of us, so we can eat together after I've showered and changed.' His hand lifted to caress the side of her face gently. 'I have a blazing hunger of another kind that Ellen can't do a thing about, but that has to wait.'

Cori forced a smile to her lips and felt his brush them briefly before going out to his own room. Swallowing the lump in her throat, she went like an automaton to the wide closet and took out a loosely flowing housegown, waiting until she heard Greg leaving the bathroom before she went to it. The scent of the cologne he used hung in the steamy atmosphere, and tears gathered in her eyes, blinding her as she stood under the stinging spray of the shower.

Why couldn't he have told her the truth about Bobby? About his relationship with Marisa? About—his brother's death? She could have understood his falling in love with his brother's wife, the fact that Bobby had been born of that love, and even the fact that his brother had died at his hand—although she would never believe that had been anything other than an accident. It was his dishonesty that made any true marriage between him and Cori impossible.

He was halfway through the hastily prepared meal when Cori put in an appearance in the dining room, and his eyes went appreciatively over the honey tones of her robe.

'Sorry, honey, I couldn't wait for you. The boys are waiting down below.'

'It's all right, I have lots of time,' she returned gravely. sitting down at her place opposite and smiling her thanks to Ellen when she came to put a colourful plate of ham slices, eggs, browned potatoes and grilled tomatoes before her. Appetite overcame despondency, and Cori assuaged her hunger rapidly, feeling immeasurably better when half of the meal was inside her and Greg took his last draught of coffee and stood up.

'I have to go,' he said, moving round the table to stand over her, freshly handsome in beige-coloured denim, his smooth chin and brushed back hair a contrast to his more boyish appearance at the cabin. 'Don't get up, finish your meal. And rest up for when I get back, won't you?' he added, bending to take her lips with the hardness of his own. Tears rushed suddenly to Cori's eyes and again he misunderstood the reason for them. 'I'll be back as soon as I can, sweetheart,' he promised softly, his fingers flexing on her shoulder. 'Believe me, I don't want to go.'

Believe him! More believable were his words to Bobby a moment later in the hall.

'Take care of things while I'm gone, son, won't you?'

'Son!' Bobby didn't know how true that word was! Was that why Greg used it so often in addressing the boy? That he used it as a secondhand kind of acknowledgement of his son?

Whether it was or not, Cori knew now that it was no concern of hers any longer. This absence of Greg for several days came as a heaven sent opportunity for her to leave the ranch without a face-to-face confrontation which would have solved nothing and caused further wounding to Cori's heart. Wounding hurts she knew would never heal.

Strangely, her opportunity for escape came from Marisa later that day when she and Cori sat in unwanted togetherness at the dinner table. Bitterness rose as an acrid gall in Cori's throat when Ellen placed before them the steaks intended for Greg and Cori earlier, and she made only a slight pretence of eating it.

Marisa, her tongue loosened by the wine she had consumed with her dinner, broke the silence at last.

'Well? Did you ask Greg about what I told you?' she asked boldly, her eyes going over Cori's pinched face with an amused gleam. 'I wouldn't have to be a mind-reader to know that he denied it!'

'No, he didn't deny it,' Cori said in a low voice, her lashes making a dark shadow on her cheeks as she looked down at her plate.

'He didn't?' Marisa asked sharply.

'No—because we didn't discuss it.'

'Oh.' Marisa seemed to digest this for a few moments, then she spoke again. 'Ignoring the facts won't make them go away, you know. Look, Cori,' she leaned across the table in a friendlier manner than she had displayed before, 'you're a nice girl, and you don't deserve to be hurt by a man of Greg Mason's type. You're out of your depth with somebody like him—you still don't understand the lengths he'll go to in order to keep Bobby with him. He'd even make love to you if he thought you were about to slip out of his hands before the court case comes up in September.'

Cori's head snapped up, her eyes staring into the dark liquid eyes close by. It was as if Marisa had been at the cabin that morning, heard Cori throw at Greg's departing figure that he had called her his wife for the last time, known that he had come back not long after and made love to her. A shuddering sigh ripped from her, and her trembling hands covered her face. Marisa's long-fingered hand closed over her arm, her voice smoothly soft as she said:

'I'm sorry, my dear. No one knows better than me how you feel, but you don't yet have the ties I have with Greg.'

Hysteria rose in Cori, and she barely suppressed the nervous giggle that threatened. Ties? Wasn't that what Greg had said that day when she had tried to escape from Mason's Ridge? That he had ties with Marisa that went back a long way—how naïve he must have thought Cori to believe that those ties only went back as far as his brother's death! Even further back was their coming together and the conception of their son.

'There's a plane coming from Williams Lake tomorrow,'

Marisa's voice broke in with hypnotic softness. 'I ordered it for me, but why don't you take it while you can? Go back to your own life before it's too late,' she urged. 'Forget Mason's Ridge, and be thankful you found out about Greg in time.'

In time? No, it was already far too late to have found out about Greg's self-seeking dishonesty. His seal had long since been set on her heart, and even as she lay in the bed she would never share with him now, she could still feel the warm touch of his lips on her neck, her throat, her breasts, and on her lips in passionate demand—passion that had swept her to a world she hadn't known existed, exorcising every inhibition she had ever had and making her wanton in her desire to satisfy this man above all others.

Now it was over, and in a few hours she would leave Mason's Ridge and Greg. The note she had already written was engraved indelibly on her mind, words which would effectively bring into play his masculine pride and prevent his following her.

'Greg,' she had written, 'I'm sorry to run out on our agreement, and to do it this way, but it seems the simplest way to tell you that it's impossible for me to stay here longer. You see, I've realised that Roger still means a lot to me—maybe being with you at the cabin pointed this up in my mind—and I think it's better for both of us that I leave while you're away.

'I'm sure you can work out Bobby's custody in some other more satisfactory way, and that he'll finally end up where he belongs.

Cori.'

Dawn was sending misty fingers of light over the valley before Cori dropped into a fitful sleep, a sleep that did little to refresh her. When she woke at a little after eight, Bobby's pyjamaed figure was standing by the bed and she blinked owlishly, thinking she was still in the clutch of the fragmentary dreams she had been having. But his voice was real enough when he said accusingly:

'Mommy says you're leaving! It's not true, is it, Cori?'

Cori sat up and pushed the hair from her face. 'Yes, Bobby, it's true,' she said quietly.

'But why?' he cried, tears rushing to gather in his eyes. 'Why do you want to go away and leave us? I love you, and Uncle Greg loves you an awful lot. You're *married*!'

Cori reached out and pulled him on to the bed beside her, cradling his head to her and leaning her own on the rumpled darkness of his hair.

'Sometimes ... sometimes people get married, Bobby, and find out after a while that they ... made a mistake. That's how it is with Uncle Greg and me.'

'You mean you don't love him like he loves you?'

Her arms tightened round his slight body. That was one question she could answer with complete honesty. Her love for Greg was bottomless, timeless—but his for her was only as deep as his desire to keep Bobby with him.

'I—no, I don't, Bobby.'

A sob shook him and his arms came up to encircle her neck. 'I don't w-want to stay here without you, Cori. T-take me with you.'

'I can't do that, darling.' Tears choked her own voice. 'Anyway, your mother will be here, and—maybe she'll stay for always with you and Uncle Greg.'

'But Mommy doesn't care about me l-like you do,' he wailed. 'She n-never reads to me or g-goes in the pool with me—and she doesn't like the cabin, or g-going to the lake.'

Cori pushed his head away gently and reached for a tissue from the bedside table. While she wiped his eyes and cheeks she said, forcing brightness to her voice: 'But your mother can ride with you, can't she? I could never do that, because I'm scared of horses. Anyway,' she made him blow his nose and her heart tripped painfully, remembering Greg doing the same for her, 'maybe your mommy will do all those other things when I'm not here to go with you. And later on, you can come and see me in Vancouver, and I'll take you to see all kinds of things—there's Stanley Park, and the Planetarium, and . . .'

His sobs subsided as she went on talking quietly, and finally she was able to persuade him to leave her while she dressed. There was still Ellen to be faced, but the parting from her would be far less traumatic than the one with Bobby.

Half an hour later, dressed in a well-cut but sober brown pants suit—a colour that suited her mood perfectly, she told herself wryly when selecting it—she went along to the kitchen prepared for tears. But Ellen's eyes sparkled more with flinty anger than moisture.

'I've thought a lot of things about you, Cori, but I never figured you for a coward,' she said contemptuously, and Cori stared at her aghast.

'A—a coward?'

'That's exactly what you are if you let that woman up there drive you out of the house!' Her work-coarsened hand jerked violently towards the ceiling.

'But what makes you think I'm—leaving because of her?'

Ellen's dark head, with its hair neatly braided round it, tossed angrily. 'Because I know her from way back! She's been after Greg since before his brother was killed, and she still wants him for herself.' Her fierce look softened slightly. 'Cori, whatever she told you yesterday that made you want to leave, you can be sure it was all lies.'

'You don't understand, Ellen,' Cori said hopelessly, moving over to pour herself coffee from the pot on the stove. 'There are things that——'

'I understand enough to know that Greg loves you!' the housekeeper snapped. 'And that he's not going to be one bit pleased when he come home and finds you gone.' She lifted a heavy frypan from the counter and laid it noisily on the stove.

Thankful that Bobby was nowhere in evidence, Cori raised her voice to an unusually firm pitch. 'Whether you think he'll be pleased or not doesn't matter one bit, Ellen. Greg and I'—she bit her lip—'made a mistake.'

'Mistake!' Ellen snorted. 'My eyes made no mistake yesterday when Greg sat in that dining room all eyes for you, and happier than I ever saw him. He'll raise this roof right off the house when he finds you've left it.'

'He might—but not for the reasons you think.' Cori's overwrought nerves gave way in a flashing spurt of temper. 'Anyway, it's none of your business! You're employed to keep Greg's house, not his personal life!'

Immediate regret stabbed her when she saw the hurt that spread across Ellen's olive-toned features.

'I'll get your breakfast, Mrs Mason,' she said, impassively polite as she turned to the stove.

Cori took a step towards her, then checked herself. Maybe it was better for everyone if she left in an atmosphere of unfriendliness.

CHAPTER TWELVE

'FEELING better, darling?'

Doreen, dressed in a pants suit of oyster knit which seemed to add sparkle to her eyes and soften the contour of her lips, brought a breakfast tray to place across Cori's knees before she went to draw back the curtains.

As sunlight flooded into the room Cori, blinking, asked: 'What time is it?'

'Eleven,' Doreen replied calmly, coming back to sit on the edge of the bed. 'I looked in earlier, but you were dead to the world.' She looked concernedly at her sister's drooping mouth and shoulders. 'How *do* you feel, Cori?'

'I'm—all right.' The previous day's flight from Mason's Ridge and her arrival at the Page house much later were a jumbled blur in her mind. All she recalled was her unquestioning welcome back into the fold of Howard and Doreen's house. She put a hand now on Doreen's arm.

'Thanks—for not asking reasons last night.'

'Do you want to talk about it now? Don't unless you want to. I understand.'

'I can't—talk about it,' Cori choked. 'Maybe later.'

Doreen patted her hand, then poured coffee for both of them, sighing as she handed Cori hers. 'You love him very much, don't you, Cori?'

Cori's eyes brimmed with tears and she gave a wordless nod.

'Well, I must admit I was a little leary when you upped and married him in such a hurry, but you seemed so sure of what you were doing.'

'I was,' Cori answered shakily, her lashes sweeping down to cover her eyes as she stared into the steaming coffee. 'It just—didn't work out.'

'He doesn't care for you in the same way?'

'No. Please, Doreen, let's talk about something else.'

'I will if you start eating some of that breakfast,' Doreen said firmly, abstractedly taking a piece of toast from the tray and nibbling it herself. When Cori lifted a forkful of scrambled eggs to her lips, she went on casually:

'As a matter of fact, there *is* something else we can talk about. I was going to write you very soon about it, but the fact is, Cori, we're going to be turning this room into a nursery in the not too distant future.'

Cori's eyes widened in incredulous delight. 'Oh, Doreen! That's wonderful news—I bet Howard's like a cat with two tails!'

Doreen laughed. 'That just about describes him. And me too,' she added diffidently. 'I've never been mad on the idea of having children, as you know, but now,' she grimaced, 'I guess Howard's enthusiasm's rubbed off on me.'

'You'll be a wonderful mother, darling,' Cori smiled, risking the tray as she leaned forward to kiss her sister's cheek, her own troubles pushed to the back of her mind as they discussed the impending event.

At last Doreen rose to go. 'Don't rush about getting up. I'm on my way out to a fund-raising lunch. You look as if a few days in bed would do you good, anyway.' With a pat to

Cori's cheek, she left the room and Cori sank back against the pillows, her eyes clouding over.

Pleasure was mixed with envy in her contemplation of Doreen's soon-to-be motherhood. If she and Greg had been a normally married couple, Cori herself might have had the same kind of news for Doreen ... Her eyes snapped open abruptly. Was it possible that——?

A commotion in the corridor outside interrupted the jolting thought, and her heart began to hammer when she heard a devastatingly familiar voice say furiously:

'Which room is she in? Tell me, or I'll break down every door in the house!'

'There's no need for that,' Doreen's scathing tone came. 'All you have to do is turn handles in this house!'

She must have indicated Cori's door because it burst open a second later, slamming shut behind Greg's outraged figure. His dark-suited form stalked furiously to the bed and removed the tray from Cori's quivering knees.

'Get up,' he ordered harshly, one hand tossing back the covers. When Cori lay regarding him with widely dilated eyes, he grated impatiently: 'Come on, get up and tell me to my face that you're in love with Roger!'

But before she had time to move, his hand had grasped her arm and projected her from the bed to stand swaying before him. Her tongue ran quickly over the dryness of her lips as she gazed into the dark fury in his eyes.

'Go on—tell me how crazy you are about Roger!'

'Greg, I——'

'Would you like me to show you how much he means to you?'

The blurred outline of his outthrust jaw and flaring nostrils made only a momentary impression on her bemused vision before his mouth descended with angry swiftness, choking off her breath and making her knees tremble so much that she clung to the lapels of his jacket with her hands, reality fading as his lips ground mercilessly against hers, prying them open and savagely tasting the moist sweetness behind them.

His hands twisted with painful cruelty in the long strands of her hair, then went with deliberate intentness to caress sensuously the long lines of her body beneath the silky nightdress. urging and demanding until she forgot the reasons why she had left Mason's Ridge, until she knew only a mindless desire to submit to the possessive domination his mouth and hands and body sought.

Time merged with reality, then receded and merged again in the clinging of her lips to his; the woman's longing, already familiar to her, in the straining upcurve of her body; the bare instinct that said nothing in the world existed except his ardent demands and her longing to fulfil them.

Then, as suddenly as he had taken her lips, he released them and pushed her from him. Cori felt as if her soul had been sundered from her body and would have fallen but for his long fingers clamped forcefully on her upper arm. His breath was warm on her face as his eyes raked over the luminous softness in her eyes, the vulnerable tenderness of her trembling lips.

'Roger!' he mocked with quiet contempt, his voice coming through with only a faintly ragged quality to indicate the last few emotion-filled moments. Yet he had been just as moved as she herself was, Cori thought wonderingly —hadn't he? Her aching body told her that he had wanted her as much as he had at the cabin, but now he was pushing her down abruptly on the bed and putting several paces between them, his brown capable hand clasping the back of his neck as if it pained him.

Shock tingled through every nerve in Cori's body. If he had spelled it out, he couldn't have made it more clear that his mind mastered even the overwhelming demands of his body—and that meant that if he could turn them off at will, he could also turn them on when occasion demanded.

'Well, now that we've disposed of Roger, would you like to tell me why you really left the Ridge?' His voice held the hard arrogance of a man sure of himself, confident of his ability to override any opposition to his plans.

'Yes, I'll tell you,' she flared, hurt rising in a wave from inside her to form a burning lump in her throat. Her hands dug into the mattress under her until her knuckles showed white. 'I left because I couldn't stand living in the house of a liar any longer!'

A muscle in his jaw tensed and his pupils, even across the distance between them, enlarged as he stared at her.

'When did I lie to you?' he asked quietly, his hand falling away from his neck to hang loosely by his side.

'It was as good as lying when you didn't tell me your real reason for wanting Bobby with you!' she shot back passionately, anger giving strength to her limbs as she sprang from the bed and walked round it, away from him.

'And what was my real reason for wanting Bobby?' he asked, ominously subdued but injecting little question into his voice.

Cori swung round, forgetting the scantiness of her sheer nightdress as she confronted him with accusing eyes.

'Because—because he's your son, yours and Marisa's!'

The silence that fell between them was so intense that the banging of a door far below in the kitchen regions seemed to echo through the room. Both seemed carved from granite as they faced each other, and Cori saw the colour bleached from Greg's face beneath his tan.

At last he said expressionlessly: 'Marisa told you—that?'

'Yes, she told me that!—*and* that you wanted your brother out of the way so you could get Bobby!' She turned away from the screened expression in his black eyes, her hair falling round her face as she went on in a choked voice: 'There's no limit to what you'll do to get him, is there, Greg? Even to pretending to love me at—at the cabin so that I'd stay with you till the custody hearing.

Her hair obscured the quick step he took towards her, his hand raised, but he halted abruptly when she turned to him with hate-filled eyes.

'Why don't you deny it, Greg? Marisa said you would!'

'There wouldn't be much point in that, would there?'

'None whatsoever!' To hide the sudden trembling of her lips she walked over to the dressing table and stared down at the array of bottles and jars there. Why hadn't he at least tried to deny it? she cried inside. Because it's true, another voice in her brain told her sharply. 'Oh, why the hell didn't you marry Marisa long ago?' she said vindictively. 'Why don't you go and marry her now? You deserve each other!'

He walked stiffly past her to the door, his eyes narrowed to obscure their expression. 'Thanks,' he put a hand on the door, 'maybe I will.'

Cori stood motionless as the door clicked quietly behind him and, minutes later, she heard the sound of a car's engine, the savage crunch of gravel under its wheels as it sped down the driveway.

'Oh, Greg,' she cried aloud, choking noisily on a sob as she threw herself across the bed. 'Greg!'

'Marisa Mason's playing tonight,' said Doreen, looking over the top of the morning newspaper at Cori.

'Yes, I know,' Cori returned evenly, finishing the last of her coffee. 'In fact, I'm going to the concert with Joel.'

'Do you think that's wise, darling? She *is* Greg's sister-in-law, isn't she?'

'Yes, she's Bobby's mother.' Cori had filled in a few of the details of her short-lived marriage apart from her fondness for Bobby. 'Didn't I tell you she came to Mason's Ridge while I was there? She used to play to—us in the evenings.'

'Did she?' said Doreen thoughtfully, adjusting the glasses she had lately taken to wearing for reading purposes and returning to the paper. 'It says here that she's beginning a North American tour in Vancouver, and it's to be her last. She's marrying again, but she won't say who the man is as he's not free of his wife yet. Really, these people!—they're married to one person one day and somebody completely different the next.'

'You only think that because your own life is dedicated to the basic values, my love,' said Howard, the pedantry of his words belied by the openly adoring kiss he came round the table to bestow on his pregnant wife. 'And I'm very glad of it.'

'Did you know Marisa Mason was remarrying?' Doreen persisted when Howard had gone.

'No. No, I didn't, though I guessed she might.' Cori rose to follow Howard, already late for her temporary job as teacher to a class of privileged girls at a private school nearby.

'Is Greg the man she's marrying?' Doreen's eyes were watchfully compassionate on her younger sister's face, a face that had grown progressively sadder over the past two months.

'I really don't know, Doreen. Possibly. I have to go now —see you later.'

Cori escaped to the hall, tears stinging the back of her eyes as she picked up her leather jacket from one of the exquisitely carved chairs outside the door. The official letter from Greg's lawyers the week before had informed her of his wish to be free of their short-term marriage, so it was a foregone conclusion that he was the man Marisa had left unnamed.

It would be better for Bobby, she told herself fiercely, striding down the well-kept driveway to the road, which was a brisk walk away from the school. Now he wouldn't be a bone of contention between two strong-willed people, and he would be with his natural parents. Away from the nervous strain of performing in public, Marisa might well become a contented wife and mother ... perhaps she would bear more sons to help Greg run the ranch when they grew older.

A sob broke from her throat, and an elderly man passing her on the sidewalk looked compassionately at her, hesitating as if wanting to offer help, but Cori hurried on with her eyes to the ground.

She just wished that Greg had chosen this solution to his problems right at the beginning. There would have been no

need for Cori to have met him ... or to have fallen in love
with him.

From the moment Marisa took her place at the piano to
left centre of the stage, Cori seemed to float away into a
dimension that had neither time nor space, a vacuum where
she had no past and no future. Marisa's slender figure at the
piano, outlined in diaphanous black by the spotlights con-
centrating on her, was the only reality. The composed
Madonna look was restored to her face—as well as an
added something which could have signified contentment,
or satisfaction with the course her life was taking.

Joel Hendricks, the art teacher at the girls' school where
Cori was teaching, had bought seats near the front of the
auditorium, so that Marisa's every feature was clearly etched
against the background of the orchestra.

The brown-haired and brown-eyed art teacher had made
no comment about the pianist's name and her own being
the same, and Cori had made no effort to enlighten him.
Their only real point in common was an interest in music,
and he had sensed her lack of interest in romance on the
two occasions when they had attended concerts together.

Blinking when the lights came up for the interval, Cori
realised that Joel had been saying something to her.

'I'm sorry,' she said with a light laugh. 'I was lost in the
music, I guess.'

'I asked if you'd like to have a drink,' he repeated, his
high-pitched voice faintly querulous.

'Oh—no, not unless you would.'

His reply was interrupted by a uniformed theatre attendant who approached Cori and said: 'Mrs Mason? This is
for you.'

Cori frowned, but took the piece of heavy notepaper
from the man's hand, unfolding it to read:

'Come backstage—without your escort. M.'

Her bewildered eyes looked up first to the attendant and
then to Joel's annoyed expression.

'But I——'

'The lady doesn't have much time before she has to perform again, ma'am,' the attendant reminded her.

'You mean Marisa Mason?' Joel exclaimed incredulously, taking the note from Cori's hand and scanning it quickly, his mouth tightening at the last part of the message. He looked accusingly at Cori. 'I didn't realise you knew her—is she a relation?'

'She—she's my sister-in-law.' A cough from the waiting attendant brought her to her feet. 'I'm sorry, Joel, but I'll have to run out on you.'

'But——'

Leaving his frowning face behind, Cori followed the attendant to the magic world behind stage where plush furnishings gave way to stark utility although Marisa's dressing room, when she reached it, was opulent enough in its red velvet settee and armchairs, gold shaded curtains over a non-existent window adding a rich splendour to one side of the room. Marisa herself sat before a marble-topped dressing table, her eyes meeting Cori's in the wide mirror well-lit by surrounding stud lights. Turning gracefully on the stool, she said:

'Thank you for coming backstage, Cori. I wanted to catch you now because you might have disappeared at the end of the concert.'

'What's so important that you have to see me in the middle of a performance?' Cori demanded, her voice hard as she looked down into the liquid depths of Marisa's eyes. Did the woman need the final triumph of flaunting her happiness before Cori, who had lost hers? Then her expression sharpened to one of concern. 'There's nothing wrong, is there? Is—is Bobby all right?'

'Bobby's fine,' Marisa reassured her. 'But he—misses you, Cori. Please sit down.' She indicated a velvet-cushioned chair beside her, and Cori hesitated for only a moment before sinking into it. Her knees, for all her outward composure, shook under her.

'There isn't much time,' Marisa continued, glancing at the door as if she expected it to open any minute. A stab of panic rushed into Cori at the unexpected thought that it might be Greg Marisa was waiting for. 'I'm glad you came tonight, Cori. I had no way of getting in touch with you.'

'You could have asked Greg,' Cori inserted bluntly.

The plucked dark brows rose in faint surprise. 'Well, yes, I suppose I could have done that, but I thought it better if Greg didn't know, just yet, about our meeting.' She expelled her breath in a long sigh and looked more at a loss than Cori had ever seen her. 'It's partly about Bobby I wanted to see you. As you know, I've never been much of a success as a mother. To be truthful, Bobby's never meant much more to me than a reason to see Greg now and then.'

'I'd suspected that,' Cori said drily.

Ignoring this, Marisa went on: 'I haven't your knack with children, your way of handling them——'

'I'm a teacher,' Cori interrupted crisply. 'I've been trained to——'

'I'm not talking about training ... you have a natural understanding I could never have, a patience I've only applied to piano scales so far.' Marisa rose and paced agitatedly round the room. 'Bobby was very upset when you left, Cori. Nothing Greg or I did could pacify him.'

An absurd bubble of laughter welled up in Cori's throat. Was Marisa about to offer her the job of taking care of Bobby while she and Greg spent a prolonged honeymoon elsewhere? As if reading her mind, Marisa continued:

'You've heard about this being my last tour? And about my remarriage?' Cori's mute nod covered both questions. 'My first marriage was far from perfect. John wasn't a— strong character, he was nothing like Greg. We'd have been much happier together if he had shown just a little of Greg's forcefulness. I know now that that's what I've needed all along, a man with a will of steel and a tender heart.'

You might have to do without the tender heart bit, Cori thought acidly, but with Greg there would be plenty of steel and forcefulness. How well she herself knew that forcefulness, the mastery Greg exerted over every aspect of his life, his—— She realised Marisa was speaking again.

'. . . be different this time. Suddenly I want to be everything a wife should be—I want to cook his food, make his home beautiful and restful for him to come home to, even darn his socks—although, of course, that won't be necessary.'

'Of course not—he pays people to do things like that!'

'What did you say?' Marisa looked curiously at her.

'Nothing, Marisa, skip it,' Cori said wearily, rising from the plush chair. 'I still don't know why you asked me to come, but if it was for me to congratulate you on your wedding plans, then accept my felicitations.' She turned to go, then felt Marisa's hand pressing warmly on her arm.

'But I didn't ask you here for that, Cori. I——' Again she looked uncharacteristically embarrassed, and Cori stared at her suspiciously. She was acting like a girl in the bloom of first love rather than the calculating woman Cori knew her to be.

'As you said, Marisa, there isn't much time,' she pointed out, glancing at the door herself with apprehensive eyes.

'I wasn't very nice to you, Cori—in fact, I did you a great wrong, and I—I'd like to put it right if I can. I couldn't enjoy the happiness I've found myself if I didn't at least try. You see, Greg——'

She broke off abruptly as the dressing room door opened after a definite tap, then a radiant smile lit her eyes to dark brilliance and she moved past Cori, saying with mock severity:

'Darling! You've come just a shade too soon—we hadn't finished talking.'

Cori remained rooted to the floor, her eyes misting over with distress. But there was no way she could get out of the room without passing Greg, and reluctantly she turned a forced smile curving her mouth.

The smile faded abruptly and her mouth opened in a soundless gasp when she saw the man Marisa was reaching up to kiss. He was fair, close to forty, and bear-like in his hugeness, yet there was a hint of softness in the adoring look he bent on Marisa's upturned face.

'It's almost time for you to go on again, honey,' he said in a voice that suited his size.

'All right, darling, but come and meet Cori first.' She pulled the man by the arm to where Cori stood with a stupefied look on her face. 'Cori, this is Vincent Tarben, the man I'm going to marry. Vinny, this is Cori, Greg's wife.'

Cori moistened dry lips with a tongue almost as dry, and found her hand enveloped in Vincent's. Words passed her lips, and his moved too, but she was totally unaware of the exchange.

Indistinct, too, was Marisa's animated chatter about Vincent's vast business empire which took him all over the world from his base in California.

'Just imagine,' Marisa glowed, 'we've known each other for years, and it seems we've only discovered how we feel!'

Vincent glanced at his watch, and Cori moved dazedly to the door. Marisa followed her into the passage outside after throwing Vincent a placating glance.

'Marisa, I—I thought you were going to marry—Greg!' Cori whispered jerkily.

In a similarly low tone, Marisa said : 'What do you think I've been trying to tell you? Greg loves you, not me. He made that very clear when he came back from Vancouver after you left that time.'

'He said that?'

'Not in so many words, but I know Greg very well— perhaps too well. He was furious at what I'd told you, so much so that he told me to pack my bags and get out.'

Cori lifted a hand to her spinning head. 'I'm not with you, Marisa,' she said faintly. 'Why would that convince you that Greg loves—me?'

'Because he *was* so furious, don't you see? If he hadn't cared about you, he wouldn't have bothered one way or the other what I'd told you, but I've never seen him so mad!' She laughed softly and glanced towards the half-closed door before whispering : 'That—and Vincent—cured me of my unrequited passion in double quick time! But don't take my word for it—go there and find out for yourself. Bobby at least will give you an enthusiastic welcome.'

'Greg—won the custody case, then?'

'There was no case. I'd never intended to go through with it ... I've always known that Bobby's where he belongs, with Greg.' She hesitated. then started to say: 'Cori, what I told you that time ... it wasn't——'

'*Marisa!* You'll have to come right now!' Vincent thundered from the dressing room, and the pianist moved obediently in the direction of his voice, looking back to say to Cori: 'Good luck!'

Cori was still staring at the closed door, unable to draw the incoherent string of her thoughts together, when the uniformed attendant appeared as if by magic at her shoulder.

'I'll show you back to your seat, ma'am,' he said, waving his hand towards the passage behind them.

'No—no, I'm going home now. Would you give a note to the man I was with?'

She searched in her purse for paper and pen and scratched a few words of apology to Joel while the man waited, then accepted the generous tip she thrust into his hand.

Out in the comparatively fresh air of the car park adjacent to the stage door, Cori drew a deep breath. Whether Marisa was right or wrong, she knew she had to see Greg, tell him she understood.

CHAPTER THIRTEEN

THE plane dipped over the huddled buildings of the logging section, and minutes later Mason's Ridge valley opened out before it. For the first time, misgiving swept over Cori as the house, set imposingly on the plateau above the spaced corrals and neatly arranged bungalows, came into view.

Had she believed Marisa only because she desperately wanted to believe that Greg loved her? That he had spoken the truth at the cabin when he told her he had wanted Cori for his real wife from the beginning? Could Marisa's sudden change of character be genuine, or had she some devious reasons of her own for encouraging Cori to come out here to be rejected by Greg? Cori sighed. That was something she would find out very soon now.

Almost before the plane's wheels touched down on the landing strip, she saw the jeep pull away from the buildings and another question filled her mind. Would it be Greg speeding across the lumpy terrain towards them, or Hank? It was possible Greg was away ...

But it was his hat set at an angle on his black head, his shoulders in the unfamiliar thick plaid jacket, his long legs that carried him from the jeep to where she stood beside the plane.

'Cori?'

The word was a question and a statement of fact all in one. The sound of his voice sent a shiver of pleasure through Cori so that her own words came out with uneven breathlessness.

'Hello, Greg.'

As if not trusting his eyes to hold hers, he turned them to the pilot who came round from the other side of the plane at that moment.

'Hi, Jim,' he nodded. 'Have you time to come up to the house?'

The pilot grinned and looked significantly at Cori in her fur-trimmed tweed suit. 'No, thanks, Greg, I'll let you have your reunion in peace. But I'd be glad of some help unloading your wife's luggage—I'll need to take on ballast for the return trip!'

While he went to unlock a rear door where Cori's luggage was stored, Greg's eyes went over her face and figure as if committing them to memory, then they came up to meet hers with a hard and faintly puzzled expression.

'You're staying?' he asked quietly.

The sparkle of joy at seeing him again died from her eyes. 'If—if you'll let me.'

His mouth tightened to a firmer line. His face seemed thinner, the lines round his mouth and eyes deeper than she remembered them.

'That—depends on your reason for coming,' he responded unsmilingly, and turned away to help with the unloading.

While her eyes drank in his breadth of shoulder and narrowly tapered hips, her heart sank within her. He wasn't glad to see her, he hadn't as much as brushed his lips to her cheek as a gesture for the pilot's benefit.

For a moment she was tempted to tell the two men that she had made a mistake, that she would go back to Williams Lake with the pilot, but then determination lifted her chin. She had come here to tell Greg that she understood why he had been dishonest about his relationship to Bobby and she would do it, even if it meant calling the plane back later in the day to take her away.

Forcing a smile of thanks to the pilot, she followed Greg to the jeep, where he stowed away the last of her luggage on the rear seat before putting an impersonal hand on her elbow to help her into the front. His arm lifted in a gesture of farewell to Jim as he came round and slid behind the wheel, starting the engine at once and heading towards the buildings a lot more slowly than he had come.

'Greg, I—can we talk before we get to the house?'

'We can talk there,' he said offhandedly, not looking at her. 'Ellen's father is dying and she's away for a few days. Bobby's down below staying with Jean.'

'Oh, I'm sorry—about Ellen's father.'

He shrugged. 'He's an old man, he's had a long life. He's wanted it to be over for some time.'

The rest of the journey was accomplished in silence, and Cori had time to see that the aspens were bare of their leaves, to feel the crisp coolness of the late October air that held the permeating scent of pines. The windows of the house sparkled in the late morning sun shining from a clear blue sky, and she drew in a trembling breath when Greg came round to assist her from the jeep and she felt the sharp-pointed gravel beneath her feet.

'I'll get your luggage later,' he said as if he, too, suspected she might not be staying.

It was different entering the house now from what it had been the first time. The smells that rose to greet her were warmly familiar—captured sunshine in the carpets and furniture, the polish Ellen used to keep the surfaces shining, the faint odour of previous meals cooked in the spacious kitchen, the lingering aroma of Greg's cigars ...

'You've been smoking in here!' she exclaimed as she went into the living room. 'You never did before, did you?'

'I had a wife to please then,' he said drily, peeling off his own jacket and holding out a hand for hers. Cori welcomed the abrasive sweep of his eyes over her gently defined curves under the white wool of her sweater, but not the detached masculine appreciation his expression indicated.

He hung the jackets in the hall, then crossed to the already laid fire and set a match to it. The light beige shirt he wore strained across his back muscles as he bent over the fireplace, bringing a choking sensation to Cori's throat. His attractiveness as a man had never seemed more evident, and to cover the rush of feeling that attacked her limbs and left them weak, she wandered over to the window and leaned against the grand piano there.

'The valley view looks so different now from when I ...' Her voice trailed away when she felt Greg move up behind her, shivering when he put a hand on her elbow to turn her round to face him. Strange how his bigness had dwindled in her mind until now it was a renewed shock to look up into his serious-eyed face.

'Suppose you tell me why you came, Cori?' he asked quietly, his hand dropping from her arm and thrusting into the front pocket of his beige corded pants.

Her eyes dropped to his shirt front. 'I—I saw Marisa.'

'Oh?' One brow rose in mild enquiry. 'And what did she tell you this time that sent you hotfooting it out here? That I've given up murdering brothers and fathering illegitimate sons?' His tone held a deep bitterness and, looking up, she saw flinty anger sparking in his eyes.

'No. She told me you—love me.'

For long moments he stood perfectly still, only a muscle in his cheek moving slightly. Then he laughed softly, derisively, and stuck his other hand into the matching front pocket on his pants.

'And I suppose you believed that too? I don't understand it,' he shook his head and moved over to the flaming logs in the fireplace, 'you're like a puppet on a string where Marisa's concerned. If she told you the moon was made of green cheese you'd believe her, wouldn't you?'

'No. She told me that your brother's death wasn't an accident, and I didn't believe that,' she said in a low voice.

'Didn't you? That wasn't the impression I got that day in Vancouver. It appeared to me that you'd tried, judged and condemned me without once hearing my side of it.'

'I was—hurt that day, Greg.' Her voice dropped even lower. 'I—thought you had used my feelings, my—all of me for your own ends.' She looked up and met his piercing look, adding passionately: 'But I didn't really believe you had—that you wanted John dead. I knew you couldn't have done that.'

'And Bobby?' he asked harshly. 'Was he an accident too?'

Her cheeks flushed a deep pink, but she went on doggedly: 'No ... although I don't suppose you and Marisa planned—but I can understand why it happened, Greg, and why you felt you couldn't be honest with me about it. The fewer people who knew the truth, the less likely it would be that Bobby would find out who his——'

'Father is?' he prompted coldly when she paused. Then it was if all hell was let loose round her as he pulled his hands from his pockets and strode over to clamp them to her upper arms, shaking her until her hair bounced wildly round her shoulders.

'God damn you, Cori! If there's a wrong interpretation to put on my motives, you'll sure as hell find it!' He stopped shaking her then, but she flinched from the naked pain in his deep-set eyes. 'Nothing would give me greater pleasure than to acknowledge Bobby as my son—unfortunately, there's no way he could be. His mother has never been any more than my brother's wife—oh, she wanted it different all right,' he twisted away from her and went back to gaze down into the flames, 'from the first time she came here with John. She made his life hell, getting him to give up his engineering job to follow her round the world—and making sure he knew all about her various boy-friends all the way.' He gave a hollow laugh and stretched his neck to look at the ceiling. 'And the sick joke was, she was no great shakes as a woman. Her affairs never went any further than tormenting John with them—that's how he knew Bobby was his.'

'Oh, Greg!' Cori groped for a chair nearby and half fell into it, her face drained of colour, her eyes large orbs of pity as she looked up at him. 'Why did he stay with her?'

'Because, God help him, he loved her.' His eyes glanced scathingly at her. 'In that romantic way of yours that ties ropes of steel round a man—ropes he can't see until it's too late.'

Too late, also, for Cori to discover Greg's reasons for being pathologically opposed to romantic love. Every wrong belief she had had about him must have reinforced his antipathy towards loving a woman in any but the most basic physical sense. And yet ...

'You loved me—that way—for a while, didn't you, Greg?'

He was silent for so long she thought he wouldn't answer at all, but at last he heaved a sigh and admitted slowly:

'Yes ... like a fool, I let myself be caught in the trap though I'd sworn I never would.' His voice grew softer as he turned back to the fire again. 'That was my vow to myself when I held my brother in my arms up there in the hills when he was dying. Marisa was screaming so much, I——'

'*Marisa?* She was there?'

'Oh, yes, she was there,' he confirmed drily. 'She's an

expert shot—she used to go on hunting trips with her father when she was younger. Anyway, she was in hysterics when I came to after getting this——' he pointed jerkily to the scar on his brow, '... the bear was dead, and John nearly so.' His voice thickened. 'The bear went for me first, and John attracted him away to himself, saving my life but losing his own. That's—when he asked me to bring Bobby up here, where he'd grown up himself. He didn't want Marisa dragging the boy around with her, ruining his life too.'

'So it was Marisa who shot John?'

He blinked a few times and bit his lip before saying tiredly: 'It was an accident, I'm sure of that. The bullet she sent through the bear hit John too ... it was a freak thing.'

Only the crackle of the burning logs disturbed the ensuing silence until Cori's hands slid up Greg's arms and her cheek reached to touch his, wetting it with her tears.

'Greg, I'm so sorry,' she whispered brokenly. 'About John—and Marisa—everything. But mostly I'm sorry for misjudging the man I love so very, very much.' His body had tensed against hers, but he made no move to come closer. She lifted her cheek and looked up at him with sparkling eyes. 'I don't want to leave you, Greg ... I want to stay with you for ever and be your real wife, the mother of your children, and Bobby too if he needs me ... but if you want me to leave, I'll go.'

Still he said nothing, but when she dropped her arms to her sides and turned to go he put out a hand to pull her back against the smooth hardness of his body. Moisture in his eyes gave them a deep gleam as he looked down at her and said huskily:

'You've just made a commitment. Are you going to make a habit of running out on our agreements? If so——'

'Oh, no, Greg darling, I never will again,' she cried, throwing her arms round his neck and smiling with trembling lips and tear-studded eyes.

'If so,' he continued as if she hadn't spoken, 'I'm going

to have to tie you to the bedpost every time I leave the house. And, speaking of the bedpost'—he bent swiftly and picked her up in his arms—'maybe I should check right now on the best way of keeping you there.'

Her hand touched the hard line of his jaw and turned his head to hers, and she scarcely heard the two distinct thuds as her shoes fell to the floor.

'You already know the very best way of keeping me there, Greg darling,' she said against his lips.

Harlequin

COLLECTION
EDITIONS OF 1978

Harlequin's Collection 12[]

ANDREA BLAKE
Night of the Hurrica[]

Harlequin's Collection 106   1.25

ANNE WEALE
If This Is Love

**50 great stories
of special beauty
and significance**

$1.25
each novel

In 1976 we introduced the first 100 Harlequin Collections—a selection of titles chosen from our best sellers of the past 20 years. This series, a trip down memory lane, proved how great romantic fiction can be timeless and appealing from generation to generation. The theme of love and romance is eternal, and, when placed in the hands of talented, creative, authors whose true gift lies in their ability to write from the heart, the stories reach a special level of brilliance that the passage of time cannot dim. Like a treasured heirloom, an antique of superb craftsmanship, a beautiful gift from someone loved—these stories too, have a special significance that transcends the ordinary. **$1.25 each novel**

Here are your 1978
Harlequin Collection Editions...

102 Then Come Kiss Me
MARY BURCHELL (#422)

103 It's Wise to Forget
ELIZABETH HOY (#507)

104 The Gated Road
JEAN S. MACLEOD (#547)

105 The Enchanting Island
KATHRYN BLAIR (#766)

106 If This is Love
ANNE WEALE (#798)

107 Love is Forever
BARBARA ROWAN (#799)

108 Amber Five
BETTY BEATY (#824)

109 The Dream and the Dancer
ELEANOR FARNES (#912)

110 Dear Intruder
JANE ARBOR (#919)

111 The Garden of Don José
ROSE BURGHLEY (#928)

112 Bride in Flight
ESSIE SUMMERS (#913)

113 Tiger Hall
ESTHER WYNDHAM (#936)

114 The Enchanted Trap
KATE STARR (#951)

115 A Cottage in Spain
ROSALIND BRETT (#952)

116 Nurse Madeline of Eden Grove
MARJORIE NORRELL (#962)

117 Came a Stranger
CELINE CONWAY (#965)

118 **The Wings of the Morning**
SUSAN BARRIE (#967)

119 **Time of Grace**
SARA SEALE (#973)

120 **The Night of the Hurricane**
ANDREA BLAKE (#974)

121 **Flamingoes on the Lake**
ISOBEL CHACE (#976)

122 **Moon Over Africa**
PAMELA KENT (#983)

123 **Island in the Dawn**
AVERIL IVES (#984)

124 **Lady in Harley Street**
ANNE VINTON (#985)

125 **Play the Tune Softly**
AMANDA DOYLE (#1116)

126 **Will You Surrender?**
JOYCE DINGWELL (#1179)

127 **Towards the Dawn**
JANE ARBOR (#474)

128 **Love is my Reason**
MARY BURCHELL (#494)

129 **Strange Recompense**
CATHERINE AIRLIE (#511)

130 **White Hunter**
ELIZABETH HOY (#577)

131 **Gone Away**
MARJORIE MOORE (#659)

132 **Flower for a Bride**
BARBARA ROWAN (#845)

133 **Desert Doorway**
PAMELA KENT (#909)

134 **My Dear Cousin**
CELINE CONWAY (#934)

135 **A House for Sharing**
ISOBEL CHACE (#935)

136 **The House by the Lake**
ELEANOR FARNES (#942)

137 **Whisper of Doubt**
ANDREA BLAKE (#944)

138 **Islands of Summer**
ANNE WEALE (#948)

139 **The Third Uncle**
SARA SEALE (#949)

140 **Young Bar**
JANE FRAZER (#958)

141 **Crane Castle**
JEAN S. MACLEOD (#966)

142 **Sweet Brenda**
PENELOPE WALSH (#968)

143 **Barbary Moon**
KATHRYN BLAIR (#972)

144 **Hotel Mirador**
ROSALIND BRETT (#989)

145 **Castle Thunderbird**
SUSAN BARRIE (#997)

146 **Magic Symphony**
ELEANOR FARNES (#998)

147 **A Change for Clancy**
AMANDA DOYLE (#1085)

148 **Thank you, Nurse Conway**
MARJORIE NORRELL (#1097)

149 **Postscript to Yesterday**
ESSIE SUMMERS (#1119)

150 **Love in the Wilderness**
DOROTHY RIVERS (#1163)

151 **A Taste for Love**
JOYCE DINGWELL (#1229)

Original Harlequin Romance numbers in brackets

ORDER FORM
Harlequin Reader Service

In U.S.A.
MPO Box 707
Niagara Falls, N.Y. 14302

In Canada
649 Ontario St.,
Stratford, Ontario, N5A 6W2

Please send me the following Harlequin Collection
novels. I am enclosing my check or money order
for $1.25 for each novel ordered, plus 25¢ to cover
postage and handling.

☐ 102	☐ 115	☐ 128	☐ 140
☐ 103	☐ 116	☐ 129	☐ 141
☐ 104	☐ 117	☐ 130	☐ 142
☐ 105	☐ 118	☐ 131	☐ 143
☐ 106	☐ 119	☐ 132	☐ 144
☐ 107	☐ 120	☐ 133	☐ 145
☐ 108	☐ 121	☐ 134	☐ 146
☐ 109	☐ 122	☐ 135	☐ 147
☐ 110	☐ 123	☐ 136	☐ 148
☐ 111	☐ 124	☐ 137	☐ 149
☐ 112	☐ 125	☐ 138	☐ 150
☐ 113	☐ 126	☐ 139	☐ 151
☐ 114	☐ 127		

Number of novels checked @
$1.25 each = $ _____
N.Y. and N.J. residents add
appropriate sales tax $ _____

Postage and handling $ ___.25

                              TOTAL $ _____

NAME _____
              (Please Print)
ADDRESS _____

CITY _____

STATE/PROV. _____

ZIP/POSTAL CODE _____

ROM 2190

Offer expires December 31, 1979